Sins of th
-A Novel W
Niki Jilvontae

Copyright © 2015 by True Glory Publications
Published by True Glory Publications LLC
Join our Mailing list by texting TrueGlory at 95577
Facebook: Author Niki Jilvontae

This novel is a work of fiction. Any resemblances to actual events, real people, living or dead, organizations, establishments or locales are products of the author's imagination. Other names, characters, places, and incidents are used fictitiously.

Cover Design: Michael Horne
Editor: Kylar Bradshaw

ACKNOWLEDGEMENTS

First, I'd like to thank the Most High for this incredible gift. I'd also like to thank my family; my mother, Phyllis, brother Monderious, daughter Briuna, and son LaDaveon as well as Shameek A. Speight and the entire True Glory family. I'd also like to send a Major S/O and much love to some of my most loyal supporters and readers:

Loria R Redd

Anne Redapplemaleent'fam

Damion King

Andre Tharps

Bigc Kelly

Dajuan Pirtle

Roshaundrea Puttingmyselffirst Harvell (Boo)

Varski Moore

Racquel Williams

Jerry LovingLife Smith

Shataria Gray

Summer Grant

MyRe Childs

Tay Tay

Sharon Jae

Denee Young-Ivey

Debra Russell-Rucker

Daphne BlackDiamond Woodland

Alphelia Ali

MsDetra A. Young

Lafreida Putnam

J-mauel Starnes

Taquitta Nana Thorns
Xavaier' Leshea Baldwin (Holly)
Docshea Moore
Mike Sudler
Kerry Lucas
Shay Mills
Kumar Susanta
Camry Hunter
Real Alwaysaqueen Divas (Author Rasheemah)
Tiffany Lane
Shanta Sims
Love Itor Hateit
Kea GoddessMaat Thorns
Cavonna Armstead
Helen Williams
Antonio D. Lauderdale
T'sheria Perkins Smith
Paco Johnson

Dedication

This book is dedicated to every abused, neglected, and emotionally battered child in the world. Know that your stories aren't going unheard and that someone cares. No matter how hard it gets someone out there cares and will step out on that limb for you. Don't be afraid to reach out if someone is hurting you. Please take a chance and ask for help!

Table of Contents

The Sins of Thy Mother

Written By:

Niki Jilvontae

Chapter 1

My grandmother once told me that the sins of a mother can often be visited upon her child. I never understood what she meant by that, and I never really cared before today. However, as I lay here now with blood in my panties and a heavy heart, holding my big sister Terricka's hand as the monster, who bought our innocence for a $40 piece of heroin, dressed to leave, I knew exactly what my grandmother meant. I had suffered for my mother's sins from the day I was brought into the world. My father left because he couldn't deal with my mama's mental illnesses, drug abuse, lying, stealing, and being just down right evil and trifling.

I was thirteen months old when he walked out and my big sister, Terricka, had just turned two. He left us that day; and from what my sister remembers, that is when our hell began. Why wouldn't it? Terricka's father was long gone. He wouldn't have been much help anyway though because he was nothing but another crack head our mother had sex with on one of her heroin binges and my dad just didn't give a fuck. He punished me from the start, simply because I was a product of my mother. Her sins condemned me before I even had a chance to make a name for myself. The sins of my mother ruined my life. Her sins led me to the situation I now found myself trapped in.

I closed my eyes tight as tears ran down my face and I laid on my side, pulling my legs up to my chest and placing my head on my sister's shoulder. When I reopened my eyes, I watched as tears rolled down Terricka's copper cheeks and she bit her bottom lip, gripping my hand as she poured her heart out in a rap. That was our solace...our way out. We released it all in a song. My sister rapped from her heart, releasing all of the emotions and stereotypes pinned on us because of our mother. I felt everything she said as she let go of her pain.

"Don't nobody give a fuck about a bitch like me,
I was raised by a junky what you think I'ma be.
A hoe just like my mama what the hood always said,
Or maybe I'll get my bank up being a rat, to the Feds.
She gonna be just like ha mama, another roguish ass bitch,

Or like Pookie on New Jack City sucking on a glass dick.
Everybody had me figure out, everybody but me,
Cause when I looked in the mirror that's the shit I never could see.
Wasn't nobody crying at night with me and Tisha in bed,
You can't feel my fucking pain or see the tears that I shed.
I just want out of this shit, no more selling my soul.
I keeping praying to God for help while watching mayhem unfold.
It's gotta get better one day, but what do I tell my brother right now,
When he asks what's going on and he wonna know how?
How a mother who gave us life could cause us so much pain?
I don't think 1000 years could erase the shit from my brain.
So, I'm crashing out, fuck the world it's just Tish and my brother,
I'm forever a cursed child carrying the sins of thy mother!"

Terricka rapped with so much pain and passion tears poured from my eyes and my words got stuck in my throat as I tried to sing the chorus to the song.

"Terricka, I don't think I can do this." I said in a cracked, raspy voice barely above a whisper.

"Just take your time lil sis. Let it all out in the song." Terricka said to me as she reached over and wiped away some of my tears.

At that very moment I felt all of the pain and anger I experienced every time I was beaten, abused, or mistreated because of my mother, because of something she did or didn't do. Before long, I felt emotion take over me and my mouth opened, releasing every bit of pain, hurt, heartache, anxiety, and fear I had inside. I felt free at that moment.

"Nobody understands how it feels to be a cursed child,
Nobody even cares when you lie, rebel, and run wild.
It's a cold, cruel world when you don't have the love and care from others,
But the pain goes deep, carrying the sins of thy mother!"

I sang as I squeezed my eyes shut and tears ran down my cheeks.

I opened my eyes and looked into my sister's sad, critical face as my heart raced in my chest. Somehow I knew that our pain for that day wasn't over with yet. I could feel that there was more to come and that thought made me just want to pull myself inside of myself and die.

"Maine Tisha, has mama lost her fucking mind? The little bit she had anyway. Why did she refuse inpatient treatment and lie like she takes those meds? Mama is fucking sick in the head Tisha and she is gonna kill us, eventually. I can't let her do that though…I'll kill that crazy bitch first, I promise…. I just hate her, Tisha. I hate her with all of me!" My big sister Terricka cried as I pulled her closer to me and we laid in the bed, head-to-head, tears-to-tears like we'd done all of our lives.

I understood Terricka's feelings and thoughts completely. I often found myself hating our mama because of the shit she did too, but unlike Terricka I always forgave her and tried to rationalize her behavior. I don't know why I always tried to find the silver lining in everything, but I did. I think I did it to keep myself sane because if I let the hate and anger inside of me out it wasn't no telling what I would do. My sister was the opposite though. Terricka was the hot head, the gangsta. She didn't give a fuck about anything in life but me and our little brother, Shamel, whom we called Sha for short. Terricka didn't give a fuck that our mama was clearly bipolar, schizophrenic, and a manic depressant.

All Terricka saw when she looked at our mama was the woman who beat us mercilessly since we were two years old. The woman who starved us for days on end and kept us home from school sometimes just to torture us, physically and mentally. My mother, Denise, was also that woman who submerged our little brother, Sha, in a tub of scolding hot water when he was sixteen months old, leaving a burn up his left leg all the way to his chest, which was still visible even though he was ten years old.

She was the reason he rarely spoke and didn't trust anyone but me and Terricka. My mother was the woman who was supposed to love and protect us, yet, she did nothing but cause us unthinkable pain. That is why I totally understood the way that my sister felt. I just couldn't make myself hate her no matter what she did to me. I always believed in honor thy father and mother, but I couldn't figure out what you were supposed to do when that mother and father hated you.

"I know T….I know. She is still our mother though and she's sick T. I hate all the beatings, psycho rants, and now this new torture she started. I hate it all, but what are we gonna do T? No one cares. Look how many times we ran away or called CPS only for them to do nothing, or for them to remove us and then send us right back. No one believes us Terricka or they simply don't give a fuck, either way it goes we're stuck until we're eighteen years old." I said to Terricka as I wiped my tears with the back of my hand.

I hated to admit it and it sounded so damning when I said it out loud, but it was true. No one cared about what happened to us so we just had to endure it all until we could make a better way for ourselves. I just hoped that we would be able to hold on. It seemed our mother was getting worse by the day with the punches to the face and degrading remarks, but now she had taken it to another level, pimping us out like little whores.

After her welfare got cut off the previous month for her missing welfare-to-work classes, our mama quickly found out that she couldn't support her drug habit. She came to me with her proposition one day while I was sitting in the kitchen helping Sha with his homework. I can remember it like it was yesterday. I can still smell the liquor coming out of her pores and the thick heroin and cigarette smoke emitting from the tattered, dingy white t-shirt and black tights she had on. My mama looked like a cracked out skeleton as she sauntered into the kitchen smoking a blunt with her hair all matted on her head and her glossy, bloodshot eyes planted on me.

She smirked at me with a nasty, insane look that made my flesh crawl as I sat up straight in my chair and waited for whatever madness that was about to come out of her mouth. She said nothing at first though, she just walked around the table and ran her dirty, wrinkled hand across my brother's nappy head. I watched as Sha cringed in fear when her fingers touched him and he quickly got up and ran away. He didn't even like my mother to look at him, let alone touch him, so I knew he was waiting for the perfect time to leave the moment he saw her come in.

"Awwww Shamel, how you gonna act like that with yo mama…lil retarded mute ass!" My mother yelled after Sha as she laughed a raspy, insane laugh while looking at me.

I couldn't help but to roll my eyes and suck my teeth at her because she made me furious whenever she messed with or talked about Sha. He wasn't retarded and she knew it. He was born addicted to heroin and was expected to be mentally retarded but he wasn't. He was actually really smart, always reading and telling me stories about princesses and castles. However, he never let the rest of the world see that side of him. He cut everyone else off, not letting them get close enough to hurt him. He did that because of the things my mother had done to him. She had caused everything bad in me and Terricka's lives, and was doing the same to him, yet she blamed him for his own inadequacies.

"He isn't retarded mama, just stop, please. Let me run you a bath and make some coffee." I said getting up and heading over to the stove to put on a pot of water.

I could feel my mother's eyes on my back as I turned on the burner and put the pot of water I filled up on it while she continued to laugh, causing the hair on the back of my neck to stand up.

"Awww Shartisha doesn't like when I talk about her lil retarded brother, huh? I'm supposed to just ignore the fact that the lil faggot is ten years old and won't talk. He won't talk to me or anybody else, nobody, but you and your sister anyway. Oh, so that's normal, huh? Fuck that, that muthafucka is retarded…a damn Radio." My mother said laughing as I looked down at the boiling water in the pot while biting my bottom lip, holding my rage inside.

A part of me just wanted to turn around and punch her right in her fucking face, but I knew how that would end. Terricka had tried that once and my mother broke her hand by hitting her with a metal bat as she blocked her head. I knew my mother was too crazy and reckless to buck like that so like always, I sucked up my feelings. I closed my eyes and listened to the lyrics of our salvation song in my head as my mother continued to rage. I must have zoned out or something because the next thing I knew my mother had grabbed me by the back of my hair with one hand and punched me in the stomach with the other as she bent me over the boiling pot, pushing my face closer to the heat.

"Now listen here lil bitch, don't you ever tune me out like what I'm saying is irrelevant. I run this, I run you. That lil fucker is retarded and you and Shaterricka are some lazy, little, ungrateful bitches, but guess what? All that shit finna end. Now, my shit got cut off so in order for US to keep a roof over our heads you lil bitches going to pull y'all weight. That means what the fuck I say goes. Do you understand me, Shartisha?" My mother yelled at me as she pushed my face so close to the boiling water I could feel the steam sear my skin.

I struggled in my mama's grip as she pushed me closer to the water and my body began to tremble. I couldn't imagine a parent doing something so hateful to their child as tears fell from my eyes into the boiling pot that my mother was about to drown me in. It was my worst nightmare coming true and I couldn't get out of it. I knew I had to go along with whatever she said to save myself. I had to do what I always did, surrender.

"So starting in a couple of weeks Sharterricka and you will joining in the family business." My mama said before laughing as I gave her a crazy look out of the corner of my eye as she continued to hold my face over the pot.

I couldn't understand what business she was talking about. I tried hard to figure out what business she meant, the being a crazy, evil bitch business or the thieving junky business. I wanted no parts of either of them; however, something inside told me that neither of them were what my mother was talking about.

"I'm going to put a bell outside of y'all door to let y'all know when to get ready. I will send up customers that don't want me, but are looking for something younger and you and your sister will do whatever they want. I don't want to hear no shit either Tisha because y'all heifas owe me. I sacrificed everything to have y'all asses and now it's time you pay me back. Remember, I see and hear everything too, Tisha, the robots tell me everything so if you try to get help or sabotage my shit in any way you will suffer. I may just make Shamel suffer to show you I mean what the fuck I'm saying. Now, are you ready to act right or do I have to dip yo fucking face in this pot and give you a chemical peel from hell?" My mother asked me as she held my head tighter, jerking it close to the water and then pulling it away.

My heart was stuck in my throat and I felt as if I would faint as I replayed everything she had just said in my head. I couldn't believe it, but she wanted to sell us to men to support her habits because she surely wasn't going to buy food or clothes with it. I hated her for even suggesting something like that, but I knew it was no fighting it. I had to do what she said or else.

"Yes Mama, I understand. Please mama, let me go, you're hurting me." I cried as my mother laughed before letting me go and standing back to watch me cower in the corner by the stove and cry.

I could tell that she enjoyed seeing me suffer as her eyes lit up watching me shake in fear. In that moment I felt the rage Terricka always felt, but I held it inside.

"Come give mama some sugar." My mother suddenly said raising her arms and motioning for me to come over.

In a matter of seconds she had gone from a sadistic animal to a loving mother, and that was the shit that scared me the most, her instability. My heart pounded so fast and so loudly I could hear it throb in my ears as I went over to kiss my mother on her cheek before quickly disappearing to my room. My mother's voice trailed me to my room and I could still hear it when I closed the door. I can still hear it a month later as I lay there with my big sister, recovering from what would be our first of many sexual experiences to fund our mother's habits.

"It will get better soon T, I promise" I said to my sister suddenly as I came back from my trip down memory lane.

I could tell Terricka knew I was reliving the past because she had that same lost, hurt look on her face I felt whenever I thought about all we'd been through. In my sixteen, soon-to-be seventeen years of life and Terricka's seventeen almost eighteen years old, we had endured some things people just weren't supposed to know about, let alone go through, but we survived. I guess that's why I kept hoping that things would get better. I couldn't see how they could get any worse. Or at least, I couldn't at that second, but I was about to find out.

Chapter 2

Suddenly the hoe bell my mother put outside of our room went off and I heard her footsteps outside of the door. Terricka sat up in the bed with her fists clenched and I sat next to her, tucking my knees up to my chest and clasping my fingers together. My heart raced a mile a minute and I felt nauseous as I watched the door knob turn and our mother entered the room. When she stepped in, Terricka and I almost died. There she was buck naked with a leather collar cinched around her neck that was attached to a dog chain as she puffed a blunt.

I hid my eyes and then closed them tight, trying not to even look at the crazy lady standing before me. I felt sick at the stomach just thinking about the perverse, unnatural things my mother may have been doing, and I felt even worse thinking about what she was about to make us do. I opened my eyes and glanced at Terricka, who was staring at my mother with the most hateful look I had ever seen. I knew that if my sister could have, she would have killed my mother with her bare hands right then. A part of me wished she would have, especially if I knew what was about to come.

I watched my mother from the corner of my eye as she walked over to the bed carrying two pink baby doll gowns and some baby wipes. She threw them on the bed at our feet before rolling her eyes and walking back towards the door.

"I got a high paying customer in my room that wants some young meat. Y'all got five minutes to clean up with those wipes and get dressed before he comes in. Clean up good and then get y'all asses back in that bed. Remember, the robots tell me everything so one fuck up and I'm beating the shit out of Shamel." My mother said as I shook my head that I understood and tears fell from my eyes.

Neither Terricka nor I said a word as we slid out of bed and peeled the wet, bloody clothes we had on off of our battered bodies. Our mother stood there at the door, puffing on her blunt as she watched us wipe our sore, ripped vaginas with baby wipes before slipping on the see-through gowns. She didn't care that we had lost our virginities to a pedophile that choked us as he dug so deep we could feel things rip inside of us with each thrust. She didn't care that she had sold her daughters' souls for a piece of heroin and a high

17

that would only last a few minutes. She also didn't care that she had created a hurt, pain, and sorrow inside of us that would be hard to repair. She didn't care then, but eventually she would.

I glared at my mother as I walked back over to the bed and sat down next to Terricka, holding her hand tightly in mine. Our mother smiled at us before opening the door and yelling for the man to come on. I felt flustered as my heart beat faster and my body began to shake. I could hear the man's footsteps outside of the door just as he appeared in the doorway. I felt all of the air leave my body as I looked into the high, creepy face of my ex-best friend Roxy's father, Jerome. He was a big man about 6'4" and 310 lbs. with little beady eyes and a huge beer belly.

His shiny, pitch black skin glistened with sweat as he stood there in the doorway smiling at me and my sister, looking like a fucking whale. I could tell he was happy to be in his current position from the way he kept looking from me to my sister as he grabbed himself.

Back in ninth grade when Roxy and I were still friends, I used to hate going to her house because of him and his staring. Every time I would come around he would follow me, undressing me with his eyes and making little slide remarks about how perky my titties were or how fat my ass was. He was a total fucking creep and now my sister and I had to face him with no one to save us.

"Yeah Denise, you hooked me up. Now get the fuck out of here, I been had my eye on Tisha for a minute so I don't need yo scarecrow looking ass in here spoiling it." Jerome said laughing as he pulled a $100 bill out of his pocket and handed it to my mother.

I watched with wide, tear-filled eyes as my mother took the money and mouthed the words, "Do what the fuck I said," to Terricka and me before leaving the room, closing the door behind her.

When that door closed, so did my heart and mind. I completely shut down as my sister and I scooted to the head of the bed, tucking our legs beneath us and holding each other's hand. Jerome smiled seeing the fear his presence created in us. He was just like all of the other pedophiles I had read about in books. He craved the control he got

19

when having sex with little girls. He was such a weak bastard in real-life, he had to release his inadequacies some way and he chose to do so while preying on children. He was a sick fuck and I hated him to his core.

I glared at Jerome with hate in my eyes as he unbuttoned the flannel shirt he had on while he smiled at me before blowing a kiss and licking his lips. Just looking at the long, thick tongue he kept sticking out of his mouth at me made my flesh crawl. I didn't want him to touch me with his hands, let alone his tongue; however, I had no choice. Neither one of us had a choice with the psycho who gave us life standing outside of the room waiting to hurt our brother if we didn't comply. All we could do at that moment was do what she wanted and hope that the pain would soon end. I hoped that my mother would find some other scheme to support her habits because I would kill myself if I had to do that for long.

I glanced over at my sister Terricka as she sat there in a daze with her fists clenched and her eyes tightly shut. She huffed and puffed like she was about to blow the house down while she mouthed the words to our salvation song. I scooted closer to her and hummed the lyrics as I watched Jerome unbuckle his pants and let them fall to his ankles, revealing some tight, white underwear. My stomach churned and I had to swallow down the vomit in my throat as he rubbed himself through his underwear and licked his lips. I tried to block him out and let the song take me as I felt him walk closer.

"Nothing is forever what we're hoping for,
No more pain so don't you cry anymore.
Hold your head up high and dry yo tears,
Let me help you through and erase yo fears.
We'll overcome it all if we stick together,
We just gotta believe nothing lasts forever (nothing lasts forever)."

I sang in a low tone as my sister reached over and grabbed my hand.

We held each other close and sang the first song we wrote together when I was eight and my mother had beaten us with a clothes hanger for eating two packs of noodles. Our salvation song always helped to calm our hearts and release our pain. I hoped it would work this time, but as I opened my eyes and stared at Jerome, pulling his tight, white underwear off and stepping up to the foot of the bed, I doubted it would work.

"Mmmmm… the Lewis girls. I been waiting to get my hands on y'all, especially you sweet Tish. Damn, I know that pussy good. Now, I'm gonna tell y'all how this about to go. First, Terricka and I will have a good time, and then I will have you Tisha. I gotta save the best for last." Jerome said laughing as he grabbed my sister by her legs, pulling her to the foot of the bed.

Terricka kept her body stiff and ridged and her eyes tightly closed as I reached out and tried to keep a grip on her hand, but he yanked her away. Tears ran down my cheeks as I watched the monster pull up my sister's gown and force himself inside of her. Terricka screamed out in pain and clawed at Jerome's eyes as he laughed and continued thrusting inside of her. Terricka continued to scratch and punch at Jerome as he kept laughing, ramming himself inside of her before he finally got fed up and slapped her to sleep. I watched my sister's body go limp after the slap and he grabbed her shoulders, pushing himself deeper and deeper inside of her.

I cried and held my ears with my hands as I shut my eyes tightly and tried to drown out the loud grunts and moans Jerome's nasty ass was making. I tried to drown it out and endure like my mother said, but I couldn't. Before I knew it, my body was moving on its own and I had jumped up, standing up in the bed and running towards Jerome. I was going to knock him off of my sister and then we would beat his ass; however, my plan didn't go like I saw it in my mind.

Instead Jerome raised up as I ran towards him and grabbed me around the throat with his right hand, slamming me down on to the bed. He caught me totally off guard as he yanked me off my feet and took my breath away at the same time. All I could do was gag and grab Jerome's massive hand as he held me down on the bed while still thrusting inside of my sister who was now awake.

"Where the fuck were you going my lil thick junt? Your time coming because I'm almost done with her." Jerome said kissing my cheek as I quickly turned my head.

I cried as I looked into my sister's dead, glossy eyes and watched a tear run down the side of her face. I reached out and grabbed her hand as Jerome continued to hold me in place by my throat while having his way with her.

"Close your eyes and sing, Tisha. Sing our Salvation Song and imagine yourself running through the field of roses." Terricka said to me through her tears as I followed her instructions and closed my eyes with our song echoing in my mind.

Suddenly, I felt free and far away from our heartache. I was somewhere in a field running through rows of flowers, playing with my brother and sister. Where we were at that moment in my mind there was no pain and heartache, just love and happiness. I had dreamed of that place all of my life and I'd been there in my mind thousands of times. I could feel nothing but love there and it filled me with hope that things would change. Imagining my happy place always made me feel normal again, like a child who wasn't cursed and destined to pay for the sins of her mother. For that brief moment in time, I felt significant. I felt like my life mattered. However, that feeling didn't last long because soon Jerome was pushing a crying Terricka to the side and climbing on top of me.

I tried to sing the song louder in my mind to calm the hysteria inside. I imagined myself in the field with rows and rows of bookshelves filled with my favorite books on every shelf. That was something that could usually erase all sadness in my life, but it didn't work as I cringed and held my breath while the fat blob on top of me kissed me in the mouth, down my neck, and to my breasts.

"Mmmm Tisha, damn you taste good." The nasty walrus on top of me said as he licked down my body planting his face in my vagina.

I turned my head to the side just in time as vomit flew out of my mouth on to the floor. I cried and gagged as Jerome continued to lick on me, making me feel so dirty and worthless. I could hear Terricka praying beside me as I turned my head and opened my eyes just as she raised the high heel shoe she had picked up off the floor into the air. I shook my head no just as Terricka came down with the shoe and attempted to hit Jerome in the head with it.

The only problem was he saw her just like I did. As he came up from slurping on me, he got a glimpse of the shoe in her hand and quickly punched my sister in her lower stomach causing her to drop the shoe and double over in pain. Terricka's screams rang in my ears as I tried to hit Jerome, but he grabbed me around the neck again to give me a warning as he yanked Terricka over to us by her hair.

"Look lil bitches I'm not here to fight you although I don't mind. I'll beat the shit out of both of you if you keep trying to hit me and shit. Be the good little whores your mama said y'all were and everything will be okay. Y'all just like the slut who pushed you out so I don't see why you resisting so much. The apple never falls far from the tree so start acting like the little worthless, junky whores y'all will be one day. Act right or else. I know you don't want me to tell your crazy ass mama what happened in here. I'm sure she'd be mad as hell if I went in there and demanded my money back because you little skanks weren't playing nice." Jerome said with a sadistic smirk on his face.

"Now, what I suggest is Terricka you get your ass up in the bed and lay here and be the fuck quiet while I fuck the shit out of your sister. And to make sure you do as I say and don't try some more stupid shit, I'm gonna keep my hand around Tisha's neck the entire time. One false move lil bitch and I'll snap her shit like a twig. You understand?" Jerome yelled as he looked at Terricka and she shook her head that she understood.

I watched with wide eyes as he let Terricka's hair go and she got up on to the bed as he instructed, staring at me with sorrow in her eyes as tears streamed down her face. She mouthed the words, "I'm sorry," to me as I shook my head telling her she had nothing to be sorry about.

"I'll block it out." I mouthed back to her as I closed my eyes tight and the monster entered me rough and hard while moaning and breathing like a dragon.

I closed my eyes and imagined two years earlier when I was fourteen and my uncle Scooby was still alive. Only then was I was finally able to block out the sounds Jerome was making and the pain he caused as he dug deep inside of me. For a minute I was back to that happier time when Terricka, Shamel, and I were living with my grandma and uncle Scooby in North Memphis, and everything was alright. At that time my mama was in jail doing six months for assault and burglary, and I hate to admit it, but we were happier when she was gone. Everything was good with just us, my grandma, and uncle Scooby in the house. He made sure we had everything we needed and although he was only nineteen at the time, he was more like a father than an uncle to me.

Scooby taught me all about boys, life, and love, the things my parents were supposed to do, but they didn't give a fuck about. Scooby was my best friend. I could still remember his words in my mind as I felt Jerome flip me over and enter me from the back. I smothered my screams as he pushed my head into the mattress and I bit the covers. I blocked out the pain I felt as I tried harder to remember the good times. Suddenly, I could see my uncle's face and hear his voice echo in my ears.

"I'll walk to the moon and back for you Cupcake, remember that. Uncle Scooby loves you even if no one else does. I'm all you need and we'll get over anything together. Always remember that." My uncle's words rang in my ears as my memories began to shift.

Suddenly, my happy flashback led me back to the day my uncle Scooby was murdered. The memory was still so fresh on my brain I could smell the stench of gunpowder in my nose two years later. I could still see myself walking home from grandma's house that night to get some clothes and getting caught in the alley next to our building by one of the men my mother used to sell her body to. He grabbed me so fast I couldn't even think as he quickly pulled me into the alley and began yanking my clothes off. All I could do was scream and beg him to stop as he tried to cover my mouth with his hand.

I thought that he would really hurt me as he pulled out a knife and put it to my throat, telling me not to scream again or he would kill me. I saw it in his eyes that he was telling the truth so I just muffled my cries and prepared to let him take my innocence. However, somehow my uncle could feel I was in trouble. Before the man could even take his penis out of his pants my uncle had pulled him off of me and began beating his ass. I remember jumping up screaming as I watched my uncle punch the creep over and over again with no mercy before telling me to run home. I remember running for my life and just as I got to the end of the alley I heard a gunshot. I turned around and ran back just as my uncle's body hit the ground and the man staggered in the opposite direction.

The pain I felt as I slowly walked over to my uncle is a pain I would never forget. It was just like the pain I felt now as Jerome shook and vibrated on top of me as he came. I remembered holding my uncle's head in my hands and looking at the pain written all over his face as he gurgled blood and tried to talk. His final words while laying dying in my arms were that he loved me. He had loved me more than himself and that had caused him his life.

I still carried that guilt around with me along with the burden of being my mother's child, which is probably why I never let people get close to me. I felt like I was cursed and just like my brother, Sha, I would shut myself down and just hide from the pain. I'd hide from the pain until it became too much. Watching my ex-best friends' dad dress after raping my sister and I was the 'too much' I was talking about. That was a pain I couldn't live with and I was afraid of what I would do. The pain my mother was causing in our lives was becoming so much that my memories didn't even offer me solace anymore. I still hoped that my heart wasn't too broken to mend, although the anger inside of me told me that it was.

I watched Jerome with tear-filled, hateful eyes as he blew a kiss at me and left the room. As soon as he closed the door behind him, all of my emotions rushed forward and I began crying and shaking hysterically. I felt Terricka's arms around me instantly as she pulled me close to her and rubbed my hair.

"It's okay little sister. It's gonna get better. We just gotta hold on like you said. In two months it will be April, and I will be eighteen. I'm gonna get a job and get us the fuck out of here. You just gotta hold on like me. Besides, February 5th is just two days away... your 17th birthday. I promise there will be no pain that day. I promise." Terricka said as I thought about her words.

I hadn't realized time had flew by so fast. In two months my sister would be old enough to walk away, leaving me to bare all of the pain. Although I knew she would never do that, I couldn't help but feel anxious and afraid. I didn't want to live in fear of being alone, or fear of being molested, sold, or beaten every day. I was ready for the madness to end. I was slowly reaching the end of my rope, yet no one really saw it.

"I hate mama just like you, Terricka, but I think that hate is growing more and more each day. We can't keep letting her get away with this. I won't keep letting her get away with this." I said with conviction as I sat up and looked my sister in the eyes.

I dried my tears as I stared at the only friend I had in the world, my big sister. She had endured just as much pain as I had and it was time for it to end.

"All of this shit about to end T. I mean that. I don't even feel like that old, timid me anymore. I'm tired of being mild manner and obedient. Always making excuses for mama when she's hurt us time and time again. I'm tired of just letting shit happen. The next nigga who comes into this room looking for a good fuck will get more than he bargained for. I promise you that!" I said to my sister as I thought about the knife my uncle had given me that I had hid under the bed.

I decided right then to fight back. I wasn't going to let people easily take pieces of me anymore. I was ready to reverse the curse and give my mama back her own crosses to bear.

Chapter 3

I woke up the next morning energized, ready to get out of my mother's house and go to school. I looked forward to Mondays, the beginning of the week which signified I had four additional opportunities to be away from the living hell my mother had created. Even if it was only for eight hours a day, it didn't matter, school was my refuge. I loved to learn and reading was like my drug. I would get lost in books for hours, just pretending to be someone I wasn't. Being anyone other than me was better.

I looked at myself in the mirror as I pulled on my dingy, white uniform shirt and wished I had a different life. I wished I had a mother who actually washed clothes, cleaned the house, and cooked food like all the mothers in the books I read did. Instead, I had a mother that did nothing but get high, have sex, and inflict pain on others. I went to school with dirty, outdated clothes on, and a nappy head every day. I was picked on all of the time by the other seniors and even underclassmen because of the way I dressed and I hated it.

I just wanted to be accepted and to have friends; however, my sister was the only friend I had. Being a senior herself, and a gang member made Terricka exempt from the bullying I had to endure. Every female in the school was afraid of her so even though she dressed bummy too, they never had the guts to fuck with her. Me, I was fair game though. Roxxy and her gang of skank hoes thought of me as an easy target, especially since she knew that I would never tell my sister about what they did to me. I didn't want my sister to get in trouble because I knew she was close to being expelled and I wanted her to stay in school with me and graduate.

I needed my sister to graduate with me so I just took all the snide remarks, missing books, and stupid shit wrote on my locker. I took it all in stride, knowing that I would get peace when I got in class and when I got home I could disappear to my room. That was the way I dealt with it all. However, thinking of the new torture waiting on me when I got home, I hoped that I could still ignore the bullshit. I was feeling less and less like the weak Tisha everyone thought I was. I was tired of people treating me the way they wanted to. I was finally fed the fuck up.

"Today gonna be different. I'm not taking no shit from nobody. All of the anger I have for Denise and Jerome will be unleashed on the first bitch who messes with me today. I mean that!" I said to myself as I brushed my long, thick, nappy hair into a semi-neat ponytail.

I could see the conviction in my own eyes as I glanced at myself in the mirror once more before leaving the room. The usual stale, sweaty smell of crack mixed with bodily fluids met me in the hallway as I left me and Terricka's bedroom. I glanced down the hall towards my mother's room and noticed the door was open before slipping over to peek in. When I did get a glimpse of my mother laying naked in bed with the man who cleaned up paper and trash in the apartments we lived in, I almost threw up in my mouth. All I could do was muffle my groans by holding my hand over my mouth before quickly running down stairs.

I couldn't believe how nasty and disrespectful my mother was. Since from as far back as I could remember, my mother had gotten progressively worse as a mother and a person for that matter. It was like she really didn't care about anything but her drugs and satisfying her own

36

needs. I couldn't remember a time when there wasn't some type of pain in our lives that our mother didn't cause. Every time our lives would get a little better and we would feel hopeful my mother would come back around and ruin it all. She was like a dark cloud over our lives that just continued to pummel us with storms, and I was tired of getting wet. I was tired of her thinking she could do whatever she wanted to.

"Uggghhh, I'm starting to hate that bitch!" I said to myself as I walked into the kitchen, bumping into my sister as I continued to think about the sickening spectacle I had just seen.

"I hate that bitch too, Tisha. I know you talking about mama, so I don't even have to ask. I guess you saw her up there in bed with the man who picks up paper too. That fucking lady is out of control. We're not coming back here tonight until late. Hopefully, if we stay out late enough, she will be gone or passed out by the time we come home. Sha, when you get out of school go straight to the Boys and Girls Club. We'll come get you before we come home." Terricka said turning to look at Sha as he shook his head that he understood while eating his bowl of Fruity O's with water.

"Where are we gonna go, T?" I asked my big sister as I walked over to Sha to eat a spoon of his cereal.

We were so used to not having what we needed, eating cereal with water didn't even matter. We were just happy we had something to eat, although that was still not from any efforts of our mother. Everything we had to eat, drink, and wear mostly came from me stealing from my mother's tricks and Terricka's gang activities. Whenever she could cut school or sneak away at night, my sister would hit the street with her G's and get money. My sister had tried to get me to join the gang many times too, so that I could have the protection and opportunities to make money she got. However, that wasn't for me.

I never wanted to be the type to run with a gang just doing bad shit to be doing it. I liked to keep a close circle and just lay low, drawing little to no attention to myself. Terricka was just the opposite and so was her gang, which is why I usually stayed away from them. After eating a few spoons of cereal and then looking back at Terricka and seeing that sneaky smile on her face, I knew staying away from her gang was about to get harder.

"Maine Tisha, we need food, clothes, and some more shit. I'm finna be eighteen and you know I'm put out on my birthday whether I want to be or not. Denise already made that clear, so I gotta get some money, NOW! You need some too so you and Sha can roll with me. I can't leave y'all here with her. We just need enough money to get far the fuck away from Tennessee as possible. Denise ain't looking for us beyond Tennessee. Hell, she might not even look beyond Memphis. We just gotta go. I ain't gonna get you in nothing I can't get you out of lil sis. Trust me." Terricka said as she came over to me, snatching Sha's spoon out of my hand and eating a spoon of cereal herself.

I stood there and thought about what my sister had said, weighing my options as her and Sha finished the cereal. I knew that my sister was telling the truth, I did have to start thinking about getting away. I just didn't want to have to rob, sell drugs, or beat people to get it. As I thought about what I would do, I suddenly heard footsteps over my head. Terricka, Sha, and I all paused, staring at the ceiling as the person walked towards the stairs.

My heart raced in my chest as I watched Terricka motion for me and Sha to creep out of the kitchen door as she circled around the table.

I quickly backed out as Sha burst out of the door and Terricka and I followed. My mother's voice yelling our names trailed us through the parking lot as we ran across the grass and cut between two buildings. Just as we disappeared behind a building, I looked back to see my mother standing in the door still naked, smoking a cigarette. Embarrassed was not the word for what I felt as the Freak of Breezy Point, my mother, continued to yell my name as I ran.

We ran all the way to Sha's school, not taking a second to catch our breath. When we finally did stop running, I gasped for air as Terricka cursed and raged while Sha looked on.

"How dare that bitch do that in front of everybody. Maine, I hate her. I can't wait to get away from her. Uggh, I just want to kill that bitch. Hell, she trying to kill us. Why can't I get the bitch before she gets me?" Terricka raged as she lit a cigarette of her own.

Watching her stand there raging intensely as she deeply inhaled the cigarette smoke made me think of my mother. Some times when Terricka was really mad, I could see my mother come out of her. I never told her that though because I knew she would probably kick my ass. I wondered could I act like my mother, all reckless and just crazy if pushed. I wondered did I really have that mean, insane streak in me that my mother had. I wondered and I would soon find out.

"Don't say that in front of Sha anymore Terricka. Don't worry about anything lil bruh. We gonna be okay. Just go in school, do your work, and go to the Boys and Girls Club afterwards. Everything will be fine when you get home tonight. Okay?" I said hugging my brother before fixing his clothes and pushing him towards the walkway to his school.

I watched him as he took a couple of steps forward with his head down and shoulders slumped before turning to look at me.

"You don't have to hide things from me, Tisha. I'm not a baby anymore. I know what's going on and I think I hate mama more than y'all

41

do. Hurry up and get us away from her… Please!"
Sha said before turning back around and hurrying
into the building.

He left Terricka and me standing there
thinking about what he said. The little brother we
thought we were protecting, knew way more than
we gave him credit for. That wasn't all that
surprising to me though because no matter how
much he disappeared and tried to make himself
invisible, I knew that he could still hear and see. I
hated it, but I knew that my little brother was
aware of the new business our mother had set up.
He saw the men coming to our room and I know
he heard our cries. I hated he had to go through
that and I wanted to get him out of that more every
time I thought about it.

"This shit gotta end." I told Terricka after
watching Sha disappeared into the building and
walking away.

Terricka and I went over a plan to lay low
for the next two months as we walked to school.
Terricka said if we just stayed away from the
house as much as possible and pooled our money
together we would be okay and make it until April.

I believed that our plan could work and even started feeling more confident as I walked down Steele Street with my sister by my side. When we got in front of The Overlook Apartments, which was across the street from Frayser High, my sister and I parted ways. I felt a little lonely and vulnerable as I watched my sister walk over to the dozen GD's standing in front of the apartments smoking weed, and showed them love. Terricka shook up with everyone, grabbed a blunt, and began puffing it as she counted the bags of weed she pulled out of her stash spot.

I walked on towards the school glancing back at my sister periodically as she sold drugs to the other school kids and laughed with her friends. I really envied the confidence and ability to fit in my sister had. No matter how much I tried to fit in and belong, I still stood out. I was the smart girl all of the other girls hated and I was that weird girl who was always reading that the boys ignored. It seemed like I didn't fit in anywhere so I tried to fade into the background. The only people at school who recognized me and cared that I was alive were my teachers. My teachers made school a fun, welcoming place for me. It was good that someone wanted me around because it was clear that Roxxy and her crew didn't.

"Look who it is, the skank, junky hoe's daughter. I guess we should call her the mini hoe." Roxxy said laughing as her crew joined in and I tried to push past them to get up the steps to enter the school.

My ex-best friend since first grade, Roxxy, and her crew of little minions made a wall with their bodies, trying to block my way. I glanced back over my shoulder and saw my sister looking in our direction as I got the courage to push passed Roxxy and her friends.

"Just leave me alone, Roxxy, before Terricka sees you. Just leave me the fuck alone anyway. Damn. You don't fuck with me anymore and I don't fuck with you so why do you make me so relevant in your life. Hell, you think about me more than you think about yourself. Lame ass. I'm tired of the shit so just find you something else to do." I said as I pushed my way into the building.

I could hear them laughing and making fun of me as I rushed into the building, holding my books tightly in front of me. I glanced back to see my sister walking towards the school smiling as Roxxy trailed behind me with a sinister look on her face. When I got to the doorway of my favorite class, literature, Roxxy grabbed me by the back of my shirt causing me to spin around.

"This isn't over bitch. I'm gonna get yo smart mouth ass. Hoe, you the child of a junky prostitute. How the fuck you gonna buck at me? I'ma get you though. Your sister ain't gonna be here to save you, bitch, and I'ma fuck you up." Roxxy said pushing me as her crew crowded around.

The fear I usually felt when Roxxy and her crew would corner me was gone as I felt rage take over. I couldn't see that bully bitch who tortured me every day when I looked at Roxxy at that moment. All I saw when I looked into her pimply, red face was the little cry baby bitch I used to protect. Back when Roxxy and I were best friends she was the weak, vulnerable one I would always defend. When people would talk about her father being a crackhead and her mother being crazy, I was the one who defended her.

Our backgrounds were so similar it was only right that we became best friends, and I naturally took on the role as protector when I saw how much everyone else made fun of her. Roxxy and I were inseparable until our freshmen year. Ninth grade is when everything went downhill and I wondered how Roxxy and I had ever been friends. One moment she was at my house spending the night and the next thing I knew her father, Jerome, was running out of my mother's room naked as her mother chased him downstairs with a bat.

From that moment forward, her mother's hate for MY mother became her hate for me. She condemned me because my mother broke up her parent's relationship and her father moved out to live in the crack house around the corner. She blamed me for everything and vowed to make my life a living hell. Up until that moment, Roxxy had done a great job at upholding her promise of making my life miserable too. She had done everything in her power to break me, from humiliation to exposing my mother's lifestyle. She had done it all, but I still held my head up high while soaking it all in. I was done soaking it all in though. I was at the end of my rope with her bullshit and my rage was just about to explode.

"BITCH, do what you want to. You know what? Fuck YOUUU!" I yelled as I rushed towards Roxxy with my hands out, ready to strangle her ass in front of the entire school.

I could feel my hands around her skinny throat as I squeezed the life out of her; however, that fantasy never came true. Before I could get to her my literature teacher, Mr. Glass, had rushed out of his class room to grab me up and carry me inside. I continued to curse at Roxxy causing the crowd of kids standing around to yell and laugh as Mr. Glass carried me to my desk and sat me down. I growled and hit my desk as Mr. Glass tried to calm me down by telling me how bright my future was.

I didn't want to hear that shit about a bright future Mr. Glass was saying when I couldn't see past my miserable existence. I rolled my eyes, blocking out what Mr. Glass was saying as I looked out into the hall to see my sister and her friends standing in the crowd behind Roxxy and her crew. Terricka looked at the back of Roxxy's head and smirked before she whispered for me to be ready after class. I knew that whether I wanted to or not it was going to be a fight that day. Roxxy had finally let Terricka see what I had been hiding from her and her ass was about to pay for it.

The entire 90 minute block I was in Mr. Glass' class I watched the clock, just counting down the minutes until class was over. At 9:45 a.m. when that bell rang my heart raced in my chest and my butt felt glued to the chair as I tried to get up. Everything seemed to move in slow motion when I finally made it into the hallway and walked passed Roxxy as she rolled her eyes and her friends threw paper, pencils, and pennies at me. I held my breath and swallowed back my screams as I made my way over to the north stairwell where my sister and her gang hung out.

As soon as I walked around the corner and Terricka saw the look on my face, it was on as she yelled for all her gang sisters to get ready.

"We about to smash on all these weak hoes, trying to do that bullying shit with my sister. Tisha, I don't know how long this shit been going on but it ends today. All that shit Roxxy's funky ass has done to you is about to be reversed on her ten times and you the muthafucka about to do it." My sister said as she walked over to me.

I looked at Terricka in surprise as she took some brass knuckles out of her pocket and put them on my hand before wrapping a blue rag around it. I watched the malice on my sister's face grow as she cursed and talked about Roxxy while arming me with a deadly weapon. Part of me still wanted to let it go and just hide until everything was over. However, that fed up piece of me wanted so badly to make someone else feel the pain I felt. I wanted to give Roxxy back all she had given me and end the cycle of me being a victim. I was tired of being a fucking victim. For once I wanted to victimize someone.

"Don't you be feeling bad either, Tisha. After all the bullshit Roxxy has done to you, she deserves this. I heard about all the bullshit and I'm mad you never told me. That's okay though. I'll feel better when I break one of these bitches face and so will you. Fuck them, Tisha, they just like Denise." Terricka said fanning the flames of rage inside of me.

My sister was right like she usually was. It was time for me to reverse shit. I was tired of people telling me who I was and being who I thought others wanted me to be. Everybody already thought I was a hoe, soon to be junky thief like my mother. They expected me to be nothing in life and because of their doubt I pushed myself to be a perfect straight A student, and an obedient, loyal child. Even when my mother hurt me to my core, I still made excuses for her because I wanted to be that good child that was eventually blessed.

Living like that had been all I knew up until that moment. However, that suddenly didn't feel right anymore. I didn't want to be who everybody else thought or needed me to be. I just wanted to be... I wanted to be free to be me, whoever that was. At that moment, the me that I felt like was angry and out of control like Terricka could be, and how my mother was since before I could remember.

"Maybe I am just like my mother." I said to myself as my rage exploded and I ran down the hallway.

Chapter 4

In that moment as I ran towards Roxxy and her crew with the brass knuckles inside of the rag around my hand and my sister and her crew behind me, I felt that reckless insanity my mother had. I had wondered most of my life if I would ever get it. As I punched Roxxy in her face, breaking her nose with the first lick, and knocking three of her front teeth out with the second, I knew that I carried a curse as well as some strengths from my mother.

My sister, her crew, and I beat Roxxy and her friends mercilessly for five minutes until the police and coaches came to break it up. When it was all over, Roxxy had a broken nose, missing teeth, and her left eye was swollen shut among other things. We beat their asses so good and the ass kicking was so well deserved that the coaches just laughed as they carried Roxxy and her crew to the nurse's office. My sister and I walked through the halls, escorted by the school's police officers with our heads held high as everybody cheered and chanted our names.

Inside the principal's office I sat there with my minor cuts and bruises, smiling as I thought about the ass kicking I had put on Roxxy. I was proud of myself and feeling really confident as my sister sighed and shifted in her seat beside me. That was my first time ever being in Mrs. Cunningham's office for anything bad; however, my sister Terricka was a regular in there so she knew what to expect. I looked at her and smiled until I saw the worried look written across her face. Since I had never been in trouble before, I didn't know what would happen for fighting. I expected detention or to even be sent home with a letter for a first offense, especially since I was the one being picked on and everyone knew that. I expected to be treated fairly, yet the odds were stacked against me, and I couldn't see it.

"I'm just going to say I started it all and you helped me. I'm gonna take the wrap and you will come back to school and be invincible." Terricka said as I shook my head no.

I couldn't believe what she was saying. I couldn't let her take the blame when everything that happened was because of me. It was my fight, she had helped me. I couldn't let my sister take the heat for me like she'd done many times before.

"No Terricka, hell no! I can't let you do that. That was my fight. I will say..." I started to protest as my sister raised her hand telling me to shut the fuck up.

Terricka had a determined look on her face as she scooted closer to me and looked me straight in the eyes.

"Shut the fuck up, Tisha. I am going to say I started it all. They didn't find the brass knuckles so I probably won't be sent to juvi, but I will get expelled. I'd rather it be me than you. You have a future, Tisha. You're smart as hell, Ms. 4.8 gpa. You actually like learning and shit. Me, I don't give a fuck about none of that. All I wonna do is get some money and live my life day-by-day. I only stayed here this long because of you. Graduating is important to you, Tisha, not me. I'm gonna be straight regardless. I need you to make something of yourself though so you can take care of Sha because we know Denise ain't gonna do shit. So just shut the fuck up little sister and let me do this. You'll probably just get a suspension. We

can get Lisa to clear that shit, so we cool."
Terricka said to me as I began to protest.

I suddenly stopped as the door to the office
flew open and Mrs. Cunningham walked in. I
could feel my heart beating in my throat as I
watched her 5'6" tall, slender frame walk around
her desk and sit down. Her fair complexion was
beet red and she had a tight, cold expression on her
face as she pulled her chair up under her big, oak
desk and cleared her throat. When I got a glimpse
of her gray eyes, I could see flickers of anger and
disappointment in them. I knew that she was
disappointed in me because I was just as
disappointed in myself. I had let my anger get the
best of me and reacted just like an animal, just like
Denise. I had used my hands instead of my head
and I would have to pay for that.

I could tell that I would receive no mercy or
special treatment from the look on Mrs.
Cunningham's face as I smiled lightly at her and
she stared back at me without changing her facial
expression. From the look on her face, my ass
could face expulsion and lose any chance of
getting away from Denise and making something
of myself. Hell, even getting the lesser charge of

suspension like Terricka said would mean that I could not be class valedictorian like planned. Graduation was three months away in May, and I had just lost my opportunity to make some type of impact on my peers other than the violent one I had just done. For once I wanted to be seen as something more than the fucked up daughter of a junkie prostitute.

I held my breath and looked straight ahead as Mrs. Cunningham sat in her chair with her hands together and fingers laced on her desk, looking from me to my sister. I nervously glanced over to look at Terricka as she slouched down in her seat, rolling her eyes and popping the piece of gum she had just put in her mouth. She was so unconcerned with what was going on at the moment, while I on the other hand panicked inside.

I quickly looked back at Mrs. Cunningham as she cleared her throat again and prepared to set us straight.

"First of all, Shaterricka Lewis sit your behind up in that seat and act like you have some sense. I am so tired of dealing with you and your nonchalant ass attitude, doing what you want to do with no regard for others. I don't know why I didn't ignore your sister's pleas long ago and expel your ass, but today is the day." Mrs. Cunningham said fast without taking a breath as Terricka sat up in her chair and shrugged her shoulders.

My sister didn't give a fuck what Mrs. Cunningham had to say, she would rather to be out hustling all day anyway. I cared though. I knew that the streets were no place for me. I wanted something more than that deprived, lost, painful hood existence. I wanted that happiness, safety, and security I saw in movies. The family that ate, played, and prayed together. Not the horrible, dysfunctional, abusive family I had. I wanted a real life and I knew that school was the way to get it. I just hoped I hadn't ruined my chance.

"And you Ms. Shartisha Lewis, my top student with the highest gpa that Frayser High has ever seen at a 5.0." Mrs. Cunningham said as I bucked my eyes while looking at her, trying to grasp what she had just said.

I couldn't believe that I had finally achieved what I had been trying to do all of my life and it all could be in vain.

"Yes Shartisha. I just got your 3rd nine week's grades and you made a 100+ in every class. You have the highest gpa, a 35 on your ACT, the most community service, and you participated in all of the right clubs. That makes you the perfect candidate for 10 scholarships totaling $800,000 which will allow you to go to any school of your choice. You had it made Shartisha and then you turn around and do this. Why are you getting involved in fights all of a sudden? Why would you risk your future for a petty fight?" Mrs. Cunningham asked as I felt tears well up in my eyes.

I couldn't help but to cry seeing the disappointment in Mrs. Cunningham's eyes as she shook her head and stared at me. I hated letting her down especially since her and Lisa, our neighbor across the street, were the only women who ever showed me love besides my grandmother. Mrs. Cunningham was way more than a principal to me. I told her most of my problems and she listened without me having to worry she would turn me and my family in to child protective services.

Having grew up in the hood herself, Mrs. Cunningham understood everything I was going through and did all that she could to help me. She was the one who helped me fill out all of the college applications, she helped me get my community service done, and she drove me all over the city to get my birth certificate and other documentation needed for college when my mother wouldn't. Mrs. Cunningham was way more to me than an administrator, she was my friend and I hated to be on her bad side.

Tears rolled down my cheeks as I watched my future slip away. I looked at my sister with tears streaming down my face as she nodded her head and mouthed that everything would be alright.

"It was all my fault." Terricka said sitting forward in her hair, placing her elbows on her knees and looking Mrs. Cunningham directly in the eyes.

My heart raced as Mrs. Cunningham rolled her eyes before staring back at Terricka and I just sat there with tears still streaming down my face, looking from one to the other.

"I know you already know this shit was all me. I started the whole thing, but I did it because Roxxy and those lil bitches she call a crew been jumping my sister. You know Tisha don't fuck with nobody, but every day they had been making her life hell, so I decided to let they asses meet the devil. Tisha only got involved when one of them hit me with a book and they started jumping me. So, if anybody should get expelled or whatever, it should be me, but being fair would mean them bitches get expelled too." Terricka said crossing her arms and looking at Mrs. Cunningham with defiance.

I couldn't tell what was running through Mrs. Cunningham's mind as she sat there staring at Terricka with a blank expression on her face. I couldn't tell whether or not she was about to jump up and drop kick Terricka's ass out of the chair or begin one of those slow, movie claps everybody did after a big speech. All I could do was continue to stare from one of them to the other as they continued their Mexican standoff. After about a minute, Mrs. Cunningham sat back in her seat and smirked at Terricka as I wiped away my tears with the back of my hand.

"That was a moving speech, Terricka, and I hope you meant every word of it, although I feel it is true. I heard about the bullying Roxxy and her crew have been doing today, and I was waiting to see if Tisha would come tell me. I also knew that you would handle things when you found out. I can't say I blame you for defending your sister, but you know that violence is prohibited on this campus. Therefore, I have to punish you both. This type of infraction warrants expulsion for all parties involved; however, I don't think that fits this situation. So Terricka, I'm going to give you a week suspension and a probationary period that will last until graduation." Mrs. Cunningham said as Terricka looked at me with a surprised expression as she continued.

"Now while on this probation if you get into any more trouble you are gone and you won't get your diploma. Now as far as you go, Shartisha, a suspension of any kind would ruin everything you have worked hard for, so what I will do is give you one week detention and one week ISS where you will work for me in the office. I'm going to send you home early today too, just to let things cool off. If for any reason you get into trouble between now and graduation, our deal is off and I will give you the one week suspension you are supposed to get today, and you will lose your scholarships. The other girls will receive suspension and ISS as well." Mrs. Cunningham said as Terricka and I looked at each other smiling, amazed at how well things had gone.

"Thank you so much, Mrs. Cunningham." I said as Terricka and I stood up and prepared to go.

"Not so fast ladies. I have to call your mother too." Mrs. Cunningham said as Terricka and I plopped back down in our chairs and our happiness faded.

A call to my mother meant that we would get our asses beat mercilessly for hours. My mother hated calls from the school because she feared that would bring CPS attention and we'd be taken away along with her checks and stamps. We knew what chaos my mother not having her checks could bring so no matter what we tried to avoid those calls. I had even given Mrs. Cunningham Lisa's cell phone number as my mother's secondary number to avoid those *'Your child fucked up'* calls and the subsequent beatings. I had covered all of the bases, but knowing that Mrs.

Cunningham still had our true landline number from when we registered that year, made me want to just disappear.

I sat up in my seat and watched Mrs. Cunningham's hands as she dialed my house phone number. My heart raced a mile a minute as she put the phone on speaker before sitting back in her chair. I bit my nails and looked nervously from Terricka to the phone as the rings echoed in my ears. After about nine rings, my anxiety started to pass as I watched Mrs. Cunningham grow impatient before hanging up the phone. Relief spread over me as I looked at Terricka and we both exhaled.

"She's probably at the doctor, Mrs. Cunningham." I lied, trying to fulfill her curiosity before she dug deeper into my story.

I had shared a lot about my life with Mrs. Cunningham, most of my fears and worries; however, I had never told her about my mother's mental illnesses, drug abuse, or the physical, mental, and emotional abuse my siblings and I suffered at her hands. She didn't know about the horror waiting on us at home each day. I told her my mother had Lupus and a heart disease which kept her in the hospital most of the time. She understood being that her mother was also sick when she was a child, so she let me slide on a lot of things. Whenever my mother was needed at the school, I would make an excuse that she was sick or get Lisa to step in and pretend to be my mom. I had also given Mrs. Cunningham Lisa's number, pretending it was my mother's cell phone, which is why I didn't even flinch when she picked back up the phone and called the number.

Lisa answered the phone on the second ring and in minutes she and Mrs. Cunningham were wrapped up in a serious conversation about my future and getting Terricka on track. I could hear Lisa's loud mouth clearly on the other end of the phone as she played the hell out of her role as the concerned, caring mother. Although she was just playing at that moment, Lisa was the concerned, caring mother Terricka and I never had, but often wished for. She started off as my mother's best friend back when Terricka and I were about six or seven years old, but when we turned about twelve they began to slip away. That's when my mother's drug use and insanity were at their peak and Lisa couldn't take all the madness. She was doing drugs, tricking, and living wild right along with my mother. However, the difference was that she had enough.

One day she just decided she didn't want to live like that anymore and she stopped everything. She still came around after that because she loved me, my sister, and brother so much, but her and my mother were never really close again. However, through all of the chaos with my mother, Lisa always showed us love. She would always say that Terricka and I were the daughters she never had and she always called Sha the son she lost in memory of the still born baby boy she had on my 10th birthday. Lisa was all Terricka and I really had close by so we cherished everything she did for us. She had saved us many times in the past and it seemed she still does.

Mrs. Cunningham sat forward in her chair and held the phone out to me as she smiled and nodded her head. I quickly took the phone and put it up to my ear just as Lisa began laughing.

"AHHH...I did that shit. She really thought I was old enough to be your mother. I wonder what fine, thick ass, twenty-eight year old she knows has two damn near grown daughters and still looks this damn good. I deserve a fucking Oscar for my performance for real though." Lisa said as I tried to put on a sad face as if she was chastising me on the phone, but in reality I wanted to fall on the floor laughing.

I couldn't help but to snicker a little as I thought about Lisa's petite, 5'1" tall, 110 pound, dark chocolate ass running her hands up and down her sides and poking her butt out as she spoke. Lisa really was a beautiful woman and smart too, but her ratchetness outweighed those positive attributes tenfold. She was way more ghetto and hood than anyone I had ever met. Always gossiping, smoking weed, and sitting outside on the block when she wasn't at work. Most females in Breezy Point couldn't stand her because all they saw when they looked at her was the hoochie clothes she wore and heard her loud, foul mouth. However, my sister and I knew the real her underneath.

We knew that Lisa had a heart of gold and the brains to be a powerful woman if she just applied herself. She had gotten caught up in the ghetto life right after high school, hooking up with a gangbanging, drug dealing, women beater named, Tank, who kept her right in the ghetto where he wanted her. He controlled Lisa with his fists, dick, and money, and as long as he kept her draped in name brands with fresh Brazilian weave in her head she thought she as living good. I often wished she could get away from him and find a better life somewhere else. However, I knew that she would never leave him, and I knew that if she did Terricka, Sha, and I would have no one and it was apparent that we needed her.

"Okay, okay…She fina send y'all asses home so come over to my house. Go around to the back way and jump the fence though because yo mama crazy ass got a house full of company and they all outside. If y'all come in the front gate, she will definitely see y'all asses. I'll be waiting. I fixed some Rotel and wings for Tank today, but his ass in Jackson and won't be back until late tonight so y'all can have it. I told y'all, tete Lisa gotcha!" Lisa said as I looked at Terricka and winked my eye indicating everything was good.

"Yes ma'am." I said into the phone before Lisa laughed again and I hung up.

I sat back in my chair with my head down, pretending to be remorseful as Mrs. Cunningham wrote Terricka and I a slip to go home so that we could get out of the building.

"I'm sorry I had to call your mother ladies, but I need for you all to follow the rules. I expect to see your mother when you return in one week, Shaterricka, and I'll see you tomorrow, Shartisha." Mrs. Cunningham said as we both left her office with our heads bowed.

As soon as our feet touched the concrete outside, all of that remorseful, sorrow disappeared. We laughed and joked our way across the street, reliving the whole day. When we got in front of the Overlook Apartments, my sister grabbed my hand as I tried to quickly walk pass.

"Come on in for a second, Tish. I'm just going to get some weed to smoke with Lisa. You don't have to do shit you don't want to do." My sister said as I allowed her to pull me into the apartments towards the first building where her gang had several trap houses.

My heart raced a mile a minute as I allowed my sister to pull me into the place my uncle Scooby always warned me about. I did little to resist as Terricka led me by my hand into that one place I vowed to never go, The Overlook Apartments. The Overlook, or the O as everyone called it, was like the gang headquarters. It was the spot where every gang member in Frayser hung out. I had heard of people being murdered, robbed, raped, stabbed, ran over, and set on fire in that place, which was why I avoided it at all costs.

Those apartments were like a black hole, sucking you in to never be heard from again. It was a project paradise filled with Section-8 baby mamas, gang members, and drug selling baby daddies. It seemed that everyone who lived there had given up on the storybook life and accepted their piteous futures. They were so wrapped up in just making it through the day that they never had the luxury of thinking about the future. I did think about it though.

I knew how easy it was in the hood to get wrapped up in that ghetto life and get stuck there. Hell, my mother was living proof that the ghetto could break a person down and I watched my sister get deeper and deeper into the gang each day. However, I didn't want that life. I was afraid of that life and what it would do to me, but as I stood there with my sister's hand in mine, I somehow knew that I would be okay as long as she was by my side. I knew that with my sister on my team I could conquer any demon.

The only problem was, I knew my sister wouldn't be able to protect me forever. At some point in my life I knew that I would be alone, forced to face my demons on my own and I wondered would I be able to. Walking into the Overlook and going into a GD trap house with my sister was a test I knew I had to take with or without her help. I couldn't run from the world around me forever. It was time for me to just put my big girl drawers on and face my fears. My life was already hell so it couldn't get any worse. If anything I could gain a family that would help me and protect me. That was more than my mother had ever done.

I took a deep breath and closed my eyes after my sister took me up to apartment 10 on the back drive. I tried to hide the fear inside of me as the boys standing outside of the apartment called our names and tried to get us to talk to them. I tried to be that same brave, gangsta, I-don't-give-a-fuck Tisha, I was when I beat Roxxy's ass earlier that day, but I felt nauseous as butterflies danced around in my stomach. I had to hum the words to our Salvation Song in my mind to keep from freaking out as Terricka and I waited on the boys to get out of our way so that we could knock on the door.

"Stop being a punk, Tisha... Terricka got you." I reassured myself as the boys walked away and Terricka and I stepped up to the door.

Chapter 5

"I don't know about this, Terricka." I said as she knocked on the door to the trap house six times and people could be heard moving around inside.

"You straight, Tisha, you with me and you know I got you." Terricka said to me as the door suddenly flew open and Kush smoke hit me in the face.

The smoke inside of the apartment was so thick I couldn't even see a foot in front of me as I stood in the doorway frozen. Terricka laughed and pulled me forward into the apartment by my hand as I coughed and gasped for air. I wasn't really much of a smoker so all of the cannabis in the air was really a shocker for my almost virgin lungs. I held my chest and tried to focus my eyes as Terricka led me over to a couch by the window and I sat down. When my eyes adjusted to the Kush fog inside of the little two-bedroom apartment, I looked around to see nothing but boys all around me. Some were playing the PlayStation on a big, old plasma TV, some were sitting on the couch counting money, and some were packaging drugs while sitting at the long, marble dining room table.

I watched my sister, Terricka, as she went over and shook up with them before asking the big black one, she referred to as Peedy, for a quarter ounce. Within seconds he produced what she asked for and I scooted to the edge of the couch, prepared to leave. I was very uneasy around boys, and Terricka had me in a room full of fine, gangstas with tattoos and gold teeth. Any other girl might have been in heaven, but I felt as if I couldn't breath as I sat there on the couch beside a fine, caramel complexion, cutie with pretty white teeth. I had seen him many times before at school and I had dreamed about kissing him on one of those big, sexy dimples in his cheeks. However, as I sat there next to him and he kept staring at me all I could do was feel nervous and hold my breath so that I wouldn't puke. I felt flustered and out of my mind with insecurity as the fine boy next to me sat up and looked at me from head to toe.

"Damn T, I know this ain't yo lil sis with her thick ass." The boy said as he slightly elbowed me.

I looked at Terricka and mouthed the words, "Help me."

I watched as my sister smiled at me and turned her back before continuing to talk to the tall, light-skinned boy sitting at the table. I couldn't believe Terricka was leaving me to fend for myself, but I knew it was her way of telling me to stop being a punk. I could hear my sister's voice ringing in my ears as my heart raced, and she told me that she couldn't hold my hand forever and that I had to grow up someday. I knew then that I was on my own to finally face the boy I had dreamed about almost every night. However, it seemed that outside of my dream I could do nothing I wanted to do.

I couldn't believe he wanted me or thought I was fine. I knew that I looked alright considering my hair was almost always nappy and my clothes were dingy, but the boy was saying I was fine. At 5'5" tall, 125 lbs. with paper sack colored skin, shoulder length hair, and full lips, I didn't think I was so hot. I always envied my sister's flawless dark copper skin, high cheek bones, and small fit, 5'6" tall, 109 lb. frame. I thought she was the pretty sister and I was the ugly duckling; however, there was the finest, most popular boy in school telling me otherwise and I couldn't say shit.

I couldn't find the words to tell him how amazing I thought he was or how sexy his dimples were and how much I loved the creases in his forehead. All I could do was sit my ass there and look stupid as he smiled and waited on me to say something. I didn't know what to say though. It was like my words were frozen in my throat as I opened my mouth and nothing came out. I looked at the boy again and swallowed down the spit in my mouth before opening my lips and speaking in a low, raspy tone.

"Yes... I'm her sister, Shartisha, but everyone calls me, Tisha, for short." I said to the boy, glancing at him quickly to see he was staring at me with the weirdest look.

I couldn't figure out what that look meant as I turned away from him before quickly looking at him again and smiling. The boy continued to gaze at me with the most intense look I had ever gotten from a male until I laughed nervously to break the spell, prompting him to speak.

"Yeah, I know you, Tisha. I'm Jerrod. I'm in your physics class. You that smart ass girl with all those scholarships, ain't you?" Jerrod asked as I smiled and nodded my head yes.

His eyes twinkled and lit up as he told the other boys about my grades and the almost million dollar worth of scholarships I would be receiving in May. I felt important for the first time in my life as everyone turned their attention to me, expressing how proud they were. My sister nodded and mouthed the words, "I told you," before throwing in praise of her own. I knew she was trying to tell me her gang wasn't so bad and that they were like family, but at that moment she didn't have to say it because I felt the love all around me.

"Yeah, you're the definition of a bad chick lil mama. I'm honored to even be sitting next to a female so beautiful, smart, motivated, and may I add, THICK. You are a hood nigga's dream lil mama, for real. I like you, Tisha... I been liking you for a while now. A nigga just didn't know how to tell you. Now that you know though, all I need for you to do is accept that scholarship from UCLA so that we can go to the same school. I got a scholarship there to play ball. I'm gonna G on them fools down there too. It's nothing but BIG G's AND D's with me my nigga!" Jerrod said laughing as he shook up with the boy sitting next to him.

I had no idea how to respond to Jerrod as I nervously looked around at everyone else. I couldn't determine if he was serious about liking me and wanting me to go to UCLA with him, or if he was just making conversation. I didn't have to worry long though because before I could say anything he had turned back to me, leaned in and kissed me gently on the neck. His lips were so soft, warm, and electrifying that I felt tingles all through my body as I giggled nervously and scooted the other way on the couch. I had never been touched like that by a boy my own age or someone I wanted to touch me, so the thought of having the boy of my dreams kissing me was overwhelming.

I felt flustered as he laughed before scooting closer to me, and then grabbed the blunt the boy sitting next to him had passed. I watched as the veins in his neck bulged when he hit the blunt and he held the smoke in to get higher. I just wanted to trace the perfect angel of his neck with my finger and then kiss everywhere that my finger touched. In my eyes he was the perfect guy with his athletic, chocolate, muscular body, and bright, hazel eyes. He was the star basketball player at 6'3" tall and 140 pounds with the most perfect waves in his head and deep dimples.

Book smart and street wise, Jerrod was a triple threat, talented, intelligent, and powerful. He was everything I wanted and felt I needed in my life, but who was I kidding, there was no way he wanted me. Guys like him just didn't fall for nerdy, project, daughters of whores like me. Hell, he didn't even live in the hood. He didn't know it but I had been watching him and researching his past for a long time. At that point I had already found out that he was really from Bartlett, but went to school in the hood from his aunt's house as a means of getting recruited easier. He cut from a different cloth, much different from the cursed, ghetto child of a junky I saw when I looked in the mirror. That's why I couldn't imagine him liking me.

I dismissed the thought of responding to what Jerrod had said before kissing me as he blew the weed smoke in my face.

"Damn, I'm sorry if I offended you beautiful. You're just so fine I couldn't help myself. Your neck was calling my name saying Jerrod, come kiss me." Jerrod said laughing as he tried to hand me the blunt.

I giggled along with him before extending my hand to reject the blunt.

"Oh you don't smoke either? Now that's really rare around here lil mama. I ain't trying to influence you or shit, but you'd be surprised how creative you can be on the Kush. I promise. I write some of my best poetry high." Jerrod said laughing as he tried to hand me the blunt again.

My mind told me not to grab the blunt as Jerrod continued to hold it in front of me; however; that wild, care-free side of me inside that was like Terricka and my mother told me to do it. I wanted to feel happy and free like my sister and her friends as they all laughed and watched me. Terricka nodded her head, telling me to do it as I reached out to get the blunt. Jerrod leaned in closer to me and whispered in my ear as I finally took the blunt in my hand.

"Don't worry about nothing lil mama, I got you. We don't judge here. Be who you want to be, not who you think you should be to please other folks. Ain't you tired of doing that? That was my problem. I was always trying to be who I thought muthafuckas wanted me to be. I did that shit so much I never found out who I was for myself. We don't have to live in their shadows, Tisha. We can live and just be us." Jerrod said before kissing me gently on the neck again and smirking.

Something told me that Jerrod had done his research on me as well. Somehow he knew some of the challenges I faced because even though he was from a different economic class, he had demons of his own. As I sat there staring at him, I couldn't help but to think that maybe we weren't so different after all. Maybe someone like him could truly like someone like me. Jerrod's words played again in my ears and I felt his breath on my neck as I raised my hand, putting the blunt in my mouth. I inhaled the Kush deeply while looking at my sister before the drug hit me and my lungs at once, and I felt as if my body was on fire.

The room began to spin and I felt like my heart would beat out of my chest as I coughed and gagged on the thick smoke still coming out of my nose and mouth.

"Whooah lil mama, you hit it too hard." Jerrod said as he took the blunt out of my hand and patted me on the back.

I sat up and looked at his face through blurred vision as the room began to spin and he put the blunt into his mouth to blow me a shotgun. Before I could catch my breath or even try to protest Jerrod was blowing the thick Kush smoke into my mouth and up my nose, filling my lungs with cannabis once gain. That second time I didn't cough and choke like I had done the first time. Instead, I held the smoke in like I saw Jerrod and Terricka do. I held it in until my lungs cried out and then I blew the thin line of smoke into Jerrod's face as he smiled.

"Yeahhhh, that's what I'm talking about. Loosen up, Tisha. You only have one life to live, baby, and when you're around me you're going to live that muthafucka to the fullest." Jerrod said laughing as he got up and walked over to the stereo, turning it on.

Yo Gotti's song, 'Whoop that Bitch' blasted through the speakers of the radio next to the TV as Jerrod gangsta walked back over to his seat. I felt so high I couldn't even see straight as Jerrod sat closer to me on the couch and put his arm around my neck.

"This my girlfriend now everybody. I better not see one of you niggas trying to talk to her on the streets or in school, or even looking at her or it's war. Right Tish? You my girl, right?" Jerrod asked me with a serious expression on his face.

I felt flustered all over again as I looked at my sister and she bucked her eyes at me. I didn't know what to say as I looked back at Jerrod and he begged for my answer with his eyes. I couldn't believe that he was serious and that he was asking me to be his girl. I would have been a damn fool to say no, rejecting the finest, smartest, most talented boy in school. I would've had to be a fool or gay and I was neither so I swallowed down the lump in my throat before quickly responding.

"Yes, that's right, baby." I said in a sexy, confident voice I didn't even recognize.

Jerrod's eyes lit up and a Kool-Aid smile spread across his face as soon as my response hit his ears.

"You heard that, Terricka? Now that Tisha my baby that means you're my sister-in-law witcho mean, black, big head ass. I need your mean ass to chill out with all the hitting and shit Baby Dee!" Jerrod said laughing as I joined in.

I laughed so hard sitting there in Jerrod's arms as he continued to make jokes and pass me blunt after blunt, I totally forgot about my troubles of the day. I forgot about the fact that we were sent home from school for fighting. I forgot about Terricka being suspended, and I forgot about how I had almost lost my scholarships. All I could think about sitting there with strong arms around me was being happy. Being there with Jerrod and finally having a male to want me for something other than my body made me happy.

It was so refreshing and flattering to know that someone liked me for me, not who everyone thought I was. As I laughed and looked at Jerrod's handsome face, I knew right then that I was falling in love with him. The thought of being in love with anyone and potentially getting hurt like every other time in my life terrified me. However, I still couldn't help but feel the flutter of butterflies in my heart every time that Jerrod touched me.

I sat there for hours watching Jerrod as he told jokes with his friends and danced around the room. He even got Terricka and I to sing a song as we got higher and higher and I came further out of my shell. By the time we got ready to leave the trap house, I was on cloud nine. In a matter of hours I had overcome my fears and snagged the finest, most popular boy in school. Me, Tisha Lewis, the daughter of a crazy, junky prostitute had done what no other girl in the school was able to. With that knowledge I felt all of the fear and anxiety I experienced whenever I thought of the Overlook Apartments fade and I was really happy I had let Terricka talk me in to going. If she hadn't I would have never met Jerrod and right then I couldn't imagine never knowing him.

I glanced back into the room when I got to the door as Jerrod stepped forward and grabbed my hand. I felt the butterflies in my heart flutter harder as Jerrod continued to hold my hand tight as he walked out with us.

"So where y'all going?" Jerrod asked as we stepped out on to the porch and the tall light-skinned boy I saw Terricka talking to earlier followed.

The boy repeated the question Jerrod asked as he put his arms around Terricka's neck and walked her off the porch. I watched my sister giggle and act all girly in the boy's arms, which was a side of her I rarely saw. Seeing my sister, the gangster, so vulnerable and needing of love and attention made me feel less insecure about myself and my deep desire to be loved by someone. I turned to look at Jerrod and met his warm, loving gaze as he continued to hold my hand. For a second time stopped and no one else existed or even mattered because all I saw was those big, beautiful hazel eyes and deep dimples on dark chocolate skin.

"Can I go wherever you're going, Tisha? I just got you and I don't want to let you go so soon." Jerrod said as he pulled me closer to him in his arms.

It was noon by then and the sun shone brightly as the cold February breeze cut through the thin, pre-owned pink jacket I had on. However, I felt nothing but warmth as Jerrod kept me wrapped in his loving embrace.

"We going over to our godmother's house. Y'all can come if y'all want to, she won't mind, but if her nigga comes home y'all got to go ASAP." Terricka said with a serious look on her face.

The boys agreed to the terms and we all left The O on our way to Breezy Point coupled off. Jerrod and I walked hand in hand behind Terricka and the boy she called, Buddy, as Jerrod told me some of the things I didn't know about him. By the time we made it to the back gate of Breezy Point by Lisa's house, I found out that Jerrod was the youngest of three boys, his mother was a registered nurse, and his father was an ex-NBA star turned alcoholic. After telling me how everyone expected him to be a superstar like his father and brothers, I was able to realize that Jerrod and I shared the same fears as well as regrets. Like me, Jerrod was afraid of the physical violence his father rained down on the family like a tyrant, and just like him I regretted not being strong enough to just runaway and never look back.

I felt so emotionally connected and physically attracted to Jerrod as he grabbed me by my butt to help me over the fence, I didn't even protest. I didn't say anything when he walked behind me with his arms around my neck and body pressed against mine either. It felt so good to have him holding me and loving on me, I didn't even think about telling him to let me go. When we got to Lisa's house, she greeted us all at the door with a smile on her face.

"Well, who the hell y'all lil heifas brought to my house? Y'all better be glad I'm the young, pretty, cool ass godmother." Lisa said laughing as she let us all in.

We all went into the living room and sat down on Lisa's brown, plush sectional as she asked us about what happened at school. Terricka being the outspoken one, got up to act out everything that happened as she rolled a blunt and we all looked on. Jerrod looked at me in surprise periodically as Terricka described how I beat Roxxy until she was bleeding out of every hole in her face. When Terricka finished her story, Lisa told us how lucky we were our mother didn't find out before grabbing a blunt off the table and excusing herself from the room.

"I'll leave y'all alone for a while so I can get me a little alone time in before Tank gets home. I know y'all wonna have a lil victory party and shit, but let me tell y'all something now. There better not be no fucking in my house." Lisa said laughing as Terricka and I shook our heads no, reassuring her that it wouldn't be.

After all of the things my sister and I had been through sexually at the hands of our mother, intercourse was the last thing we wanted to rush into. What we desired the most was feeling loved and important to someone. Touching, kissing, and hugging were completely different from sex in our eyes. I liked Jerrod a lot and he made me feel special and all; however, I knew that I wasn't ready to go there with him yet. I hoped I wouldn't have to go there with any male again until I was ready, but with my mother running shit I knew that wasn't possible. I couldn't help but to look nervously at Jerrod as I wondered would he accept the fact that I wasn't ready for sex. I didn't have to worry about that long though because before I knew it Jerrod had leaned in and kissed me on the neck again before he spoke.

"You don't have to worry about me pressuring you about sex or shit, Tisha. I know you not ready for that yet, and to be real, I'm not ready to have sex with you. Since I've been at Frayser, it's been easy to fuck whoever because it seems like every female wants to fuck the star point guard. I wasn't going though. I didn't even smash half of them because I always wanted more than that, I just didn't know exactly what it was I wanted. Today when I kissed you on your neck that shit became clear to me though. When my skin touched yours, I knew I wanted love, friendship, understanding, quality time…all that shit. Maine, I knew I wanted and needed you, Tisha. You just don't know how many days I've sat up in class and watched you. I love that whimsical look you get on your face when you figure something out and have the correct answer. Or how you always dot your I's with little hearts. Know that you never have to hide or change anything about yourself for me, Tisha.

When you're around me you can always be yourself and I will always love you for you…I always have." Jerrod whispered as his warm breath caressed my ear and the side of my neck.

I felt my insides tingle and churn as he kissed me behind my ear and I laid my head on his shoulder. I had never felt as secure as I felt at that moment in my life and I wished that moment would last forever. I stayed there in Jerrod's arms for hours as he held me tight and we smoked while watching movies. After a while my sister and Buddy snuck off to the little cubbyhole next to Lisa's living room to be alone, leaving me and Jerrod wrapped up in our deep conversation about our families and what we hoped for in the future.

Before I knew it or could even stop myself, I had told Jerrod all about my mother's mental illnesses, drug abuse, and most of the terrible conditions at home. Tears streamed down my face without warning as I described the beatings we had to endure to Jerrod. As soon as I finished talking, I wished I could take it all back as he stared down at me with sympathy. The last thing I wanted was for him to pity me and end up being with me simply because he felt it was the right thing to do. I wanted him to love me because he couldn't live without me and because I made him complete. For once in my life, I wanted to truly be loved by someone unconditionally with all of them. I didn't know it then, but that is exactly how Jerrod loved me.

Jerrod wiped away my tears and told me that my pain was over as he leaned in to kiss me on my lips. When his lips touched mine, I felt warm all over like I was sun bathing on a tropical island. I felt his soul touch mine as his tongue slipped into my mouth and he kissed me deeper and with more passion. When Jerrod released me and gently stroked my face, I felt like I was the only girl in the world and I knew that he was the only one for me.

We talked and kissed while wrapped in each other's arms until we fell asleep. I woke up some time later to the sound of my little brother's voice and someone shaking my arm. I opened my eyes to see Sha standing over me with a plate of Rotel and hot wings in his hand smacking away. I glanced over to see Jerrod still sleeping peacefully with his arm around my neck before shaking him awake. His eyes popped open instantly as he stared at me smiling before stretching and wrapping me in his arms again.

"Y'all can break that up. It's time to go home, Tisha." My brother Sha said as he eyed Jerrod with his mean mug on taking me completely off guard.

I couldn't believe Sha was talking in front of someone he didn't know. However, after considering how he had just found me and Jerrod, it wasn't all that surprising. He was very protective of me and Terricka being that we were the only people he had in his life who showed him love. That's why it wasn't hard for me to figure out why Sha had such a nasty attitude. Seeing me wrapped in a boy's arms, really rubbed him the wrong way fast and he was not trying to hide it as he sucked his teeth and jumped at Jerrod.

"Sha, this is my boyfriend, Jerrod. He straight and he is the star basketball player, just like you." I said trying to win my little brother over.

I knew that if anything could be a common ground to get him to like Jerrod, basketball would be it. It seemed they both had a passion for basketball and a deep love for me so I knew it wouldn't be that hard to get the two men in my life to like each other. Sha looked at Jerrod up and down with a sour look on his face as Jerrod smiled back at him and extended his hand for dap. Jerrod rolled his eyes and then looked at me as I encouraged him to be nice. Reluctantly he reached over and gave Jerrod dap before licking his tongue out at me and turning to leave the room. I laughed and looked at Jerrod as Sha stopped at the door to say something.

"I guess since SHE likes you, I can like you too, Jerrod. I warn you though, don't hurt my sister. I need you to care about her just as much as you care about ball. If you can do that, you and me good." Sha said in a serious mature tone that took me off guard.

Jerrod could do nothing but respect that as he got up off the couch besides me and gave my brother his word he would take care of me.

"Don't worry lil man, as long as your sister with me nothing will ever happen to her. That's my word! Now, give a nigga a wing or something." Jerrod said reaching into Sha's plate as he tried to snatch a wing.

We all laughed as we made our way into the kitchen where Lisa, Terricka, and Buddy were sitting and eating. We all cured our case of the munchies with the wings and Rotel Lisa had fixed before deciding it was time to go home. It was well after 11 p.m. by then and it was pretty quiet in our apartments. Jerrod and Buddy walked us one building over from our apartment before we told them they could go. Jerrod kissed me again with passion and love before writing his number down on a piece of paper and putting it in my hand.

"Call me if you need me, baby, and I'll come running. I promise, Tisha, no matter what." Jerrod said again before kissing me gently and disappearing between the buildings with Buddy.

When the boys had left, Terricka, Sha, and I crept towards our building, holding our breath and hoping we weren't seen by our mother. We had made it the entire day without feeling the wrath of our mother's insanity and I hoped that our luck would never end. However, as we inched our way towards the pig sty we called home, I knew that we wouldn't be so lucky. Loud music could be heard before we even reached our door, which made us all cringe in preparation for the worse. I crept up to the living room window as Terricka and Sha stood back, peering in to see that everyone inside was asleep. I motioned for Sha and Terricka to step forward as I quietly put my key into the door and unlocked it, letting us into our own house of horrors.

Chapter 6

We crept into the house without making a sound, stepping over naked people laying all over the floor. I stepped over a man with his short, ashy penis in one hand and a handful of a woman's hair in the other without even giving them a second glance. Nothing my mother could do or be involved in surprised me anymore, neither did it surprise my sister or brother. We all had seen that type of spectacle so many times in our lives that we had become professionals at blocking it out and sneaking in unnoticed. We made our way through the living room and up the stairs quietly before the loud, musky, goat-like stench in the air became overwhelming.

I had to hold my hand over my nose and mouth to keep from vomiting as we opened Sha's door and saw where the smell was coming from. Inside was my mother and three other naked, nasty crack head women laying in the bed wrapped up in his Spiderman covers. There were oils, sex toys, and body parts everywhere I looked, along with a video camera and lights set up at the foot of the bed. I kind of threw up in my mouth when I noticed my mother had on a big, pink strap-on penis attached to her waist and the lady that lived next door to us was still on top of her with the piece of plastic stuck up her anus. I fought the waves of nausea taking over my body as I quickly covered Sha's eyes, pushing him out of the room before grabbing him some clothes for the next day from the pile of clothes on the floor.

I shook my head in disgust and hatred as I eyed the worthless piece of shit I called a mother before exiting the room. As I closed the door behind me, I wished that I could just make it all disappear. Like many times before in my life, I wished that my mother would just die in her sleep and end our turmoil for good. I knew that I would never be that lucky though, so I simply said a prayer asking God to forgive me for my evil thoughts and protect me and my siblings before rushing to my room.

Inside I whispered in Terricka's ear, telling her about everything I saw as Sha made himself a pallet on the floor. Once Sha was asleep, Terricka and I talked about how much we hated our mother, what we would do when we were on our own, and what our futures would be like with our new boyfriends. We talked about how good it felt to be loved until about 3 a.m. when our bodies gave out on us.

That night I went to sleep with a smile on my face and love in my heart for the first time, knowing that there was someone in the world besides my sister and brother who cared about me. I dreamed the happiest dreams I had ever dreamed in my life as I saw Jerrod and I walking down the aisle together. I could see his handsome face as he stood there before me with his white tux on professing his love. It felt so real as Jerrod held me in his arms and kissed me in my dream. Somehow, I must've reached out rom him in my sleep because the next thing I knew there was a searing pain in my hand that caused my eyes to immediately snap open.

I opened my eyes and focused them, looking directly into the high, enraged, insane face of my mother as she sliced into my skin with the extension cord in her hand. The searing pain from the lashes sent jolts of agony through my body as I reached out for the blanket to cover myself. However, there was no blanket on the bed because my mother had thrown it on the floor before she started beating us. All I could do was cover my face and cower besides my sister who was now awake and screaming out in pain with me. Our mother poured water on us from the water bottle in her left hand and beat us with the right while cursing and declaring how much she hated us.

"You funky bitches at school fighting, huh? Got muthafuckas from the school calling me and shit! You hoes better hope they don't call the DHS or CPS because if my stamps get cut off too, I'm beating y'all bitches to death. I hate you ugly muthafuckas, but y'all gone learn today!" My mother raged as she beat my sister across her head and back as she tried to squirm to get out of the bed.

I shielded my sister with my body, taking all of the licks on my arms and chest as she crawled out of the bed to hide.

"Where you going you little smart mouth, wonna-be-tough hoe? You the one I really wonna stomp the fuck out. I know everything is yo fault, hoe, and that's why I'm gonna beat you the worse. You kicked out, huh hoe? You thought I didn't know, huh, but I know everything bitch. My robots tell me everything, I see every fucking thing you do. At school like you tough getting kicked out and shit! Well, its Friday, bitch, and you getting the fuck up outta here, but not before I give yo ass something to remember!" My mother said, grabbing Terricka by her hair as she crawled across the floor, pulling her back to the bed.

The licks my mother hit my sister with echoed in my mind as they sliced through the air with precision. She beat Terricka all over her back, head, and face as she squirmed and tried to cover her body with her hands. I could hear Sha crying from under the bed as I got up and tried to grab the extension cord out of my mother's hand. My sister gagged on her spit and blood while crying as my mother moved the cord out of my reach before grabbing me by my hair and pulling me to the floor too.

My mother's strength and anger caught me off guard as she flipped me like a baby and put her foot in my throat. I could feel my eyes bulge out of my head as my mother pressed her heel into my windpipe and continued to beat me. Denise beat me and Terricka so hard and for so long we couldn't even cry anymore by the time she was done. All we could do was lay there wrapped in each other's arms, sobbing as blood poured from the cuts and gashes all over our bodies.

When my mother had satisfied her anger and desire to inflict pain on us, she simply walked out of the bedroom, closing the door behind her. I sobbed on Terricka's shoulder as she moaned lightly and blood ran down my arms and legs while my head banged like a midget was sitting on my brain playing the drums. Despite the physical, mental, and emotional pain we were in, my brother, sister, and I all remained still and quiet after our mother closed the door because we knew she was still lurking on the other side, waiting to hear us say something. After about two minutes, we could hear her footsteps as she slowly walked away cursing while flicking her lighter to light her cigarette.

"I know you muthafuckas wonna talk about how much y'all hate me and want y'all daddies, but I don't give a fuck! I hate y'all asses too! And it's obvious that y'all daddies hate y'all too! Them bitches ain't here is they. All of em some worthless muthafuckas just like they seeds and I can't stand none of ya! Am I supposed to care that y'all hate me? Hell naw! All I care about is ya getting the fuck up out of my house so you bitches better hurry up!" My mother yelled as Terricka and I sat up and helped each other up off the floor.

When I looked at my sister's face, I couldn't help but gasp. Her face was bruised and swollen like she had fell face first out of a moving car. Her right eye was purple and badly swollen and we both had welts and gashes from head to toe. I got a glimpse of my bruised and battered face in the small mirror on our dresser and I almost cried at what I saw. My eye was swollen just like Terricka's, my paper sack colored skin was red and bruised, and my neck, chest, and arms had deep, bloody welts all over them.

"Oh my God, look at us T!" I cried as my sister went over to pull Sha from under the bed as he cried.

I turned to hug my sister and brother as we all stood in the middle of the floor wrapped in an embrace. Too many times before we had been in that same position, trying to comfort one another after our mother had tried so hard to break us down. Like always, she swooped in to destroy and we were left to pick up the pieces after the storm was over. It seemed our pain and heartache was never ending as long as our mother was around. I hoped that the storm would soon be over for good, no matter what it took to get it that way.

"It's gonna be okay, y'all. Get dressed fast and let's go to school. Sha, we will get you there early enough to eat breakfast because I'm not stopping in her kitchen. I just want to get as far the fuck away from here as possible." My sister said as she went over to the mirror and began cleaning the blood off of her face with a sock.

"I gotta make about $500 today because I can't take this shit here much longer. I'ma have enough saved up to get us all the way to North Carolina by the time April gets here. As soon as midnight hits that night, I'm out of here. I'll stay close by so if y'all need me I can come running; and as soon as you graduate in May, we're gone and we're never looking back. Once I'm gone, I never want to see her again…Ever!" Terricka said as she continued to clean the wounds on her face and Sha and I watched her while slipping on our dingy, wrinkled clothes.

Once we were dressed, Terricka fixed her and my makeup so that our black eyes, cuts, and bruises weren't all that noticeable before we slipped out of our room. On the landing, I looked into my mother's room and noticed a pair of blue Timberlands laying at the foot of the bed. I thought I recognized the boots and the voice I heard moaning coming from the room; however, I quickly dismissed the thought as Terricka pulled me towards the steps.

"Fuck her, Tisha, and whatever she does. You have to stop caring about her so much when it's apparent she doesn't give a shit about us. We have to live for US from now on. We all we got." Terricka said to me with a serious look on her face.

I hugged my sister, holding her tightly as I wished I could erase all of her pain. I knew that she held the most hurt, anger, and resentment for my mother because she was around longer, and endured more pain. That is why she acted out so much. She once told me that she would rather be in juvenile than with our mother. That is why when I was thirteen years old and she had just turned fourteen years old, she ran away a total of 46 times in one year.

It was like every time I turned around my sister was gone and the police were out looking for her and bringing her back home. Never once did they ask her why she was running away or even investigate our home to see why our mother was never the one to report her missing, unless it was close to her welfare recertification date. Authorities had let us down just as much as our mother and that had made my sister cold and unforgiving. That is why when she got in a dark place people often avoided her, me included. I knew that sometimes my sister's hate would boil over and she could become just as insane and terrifying as my mother.

I could see that same deep anguish and insane rage burning inside of her at that moment as she snatched opened the kitchen door and burst out of it like an animal. Sha and I trailed closely behind Terricka with our heads down, not saying a word until we got in front of his school. At the sidewalk, Sha hugged me tight and touched the huge bruise on my face before telling me how much he loved me. I told him I loved him back as I watched him walk over to Terricka, who was puffing hard with anger on a Newport. Sha stood there in front of Terricka for a few seconds, just staring up into her face before suddenly reaching up and wiping away the tears that were streaming down her cheeks.

"I love you too, Terricka, more than you know. Please be okay for us." Sha said as Terricka slowly looked down at him.

My brother knew what Terricka's anger could bring and I could tell he was afraid of it. He had seen her at her worse before just like I had, and he knew that with both her and my mother raging, things wouldn't end well. He knew he had to make her see that having us by her side was all she really needed.

I watched as my sister's shoulders began to relax and the pain on her face slowly disappeared. She reached down and hugged Sha tightly in her arms before kissing him on the forehead and messing up his hair like she always did.

"I'm okay, lil twerp, now get in that school and make them straight A's. Go to the Boys & Girls Club after school and we'll come get you before we go home." Terricka said as Sha stopped to turn around and look at us with his face scrunched up.

I knew that he was looking at my sister and me crazy because we had told him the same thing the day before, but ended up falling asleep with our boyfriends, leaving him to get home on his own. I apologized to him again for that before kissing him on the forehead as two boys his age walked up and he pushed me away.

"Okay, that's enough, Tisha. Just be there to get me. Or else!" Sha said showing me his little fist as Terricka and I began to laugh.

"We got you macho man. We promise we'll be there Sha." Terricka said as we both continued laughing while watching Sha and his friends walk into the building.

Once Sha was in the school, my sister and I walked on to school in deep conversation about what we would do that day.

"So what are you gonna do all day, T? Please, don't do anything to get yourself in any more trouble. The last thing I need is for you to get locked up leaving me and Sha alone with Denise. I'd probably have to kill her crazy ass then." I said to Terricka joking, but inside I knew that was a real possibility.

I knew that being that my sister already had a record it would be easy for her to get flapped if she was out breaking in houses, selling dope, or simply standing on the block when she was supposed to be at school. I also knew that her going to jail would mean Denise would take all of her anger and frustration out on me and Sha, and that would end badly. I was growing more and more tired of her bullshit with each passing day and I could feel my hate for her grow every time I thought of the things she did to us and made us do. I knew that if I felt it necessary, I could kill my mother without remorse and the thought of that scared me to death.

"Look Tisha, I'm going to be okay. All I'm doing today is packaging, selling a lil weed to designated people, and selling merchandise out of the trap, nothing else. I will be right here when you get out of school and we'll come back over here so I can get my money, go get Sha, and then get us something to eat before we go home. Everything gonna be straight, I'm telling you." My sister reassured me as we walked up to the gate in front of the Overlooks.

As soon as we stopped in front of the group of boys standing at the gate, my heart began to race and my throat got dry. I instantly noticed Jerrod standing near the back of the crowd puffing a blunt as his eyes met mine and we both smiled. I tried to act unbothered by his presence as I walked on passed the entrance in the direction of the school. Before I could get ten steps away, I could hear Jerrod calling my name as he ran up behind me.

"Tisha baby, where you going?" Jerrod said as he jogged up behind me and put his arms around my shoulders before kissing me all over my ear and neck.

I shivered in his arms as the soft touch of his warm, wet, juicy lips sent quivers all down my spine. I couldn't help but to giggle as he nibbled on my ear as he whispered sweet nothings.

"I dreamed about your fine ass all night long. All I could see when I closed my eyes was your flawless, paper sack colored skin and those big, beautiful brown eyes. I ain't gonna lie, Tisha, I think I'm falling in love witcha girl. What kinda voodoo did you put on me?" Jerrod asked joking as he continued to nibble on my neck and tickle me from behind.

I laughed and squirmed in his arms until he suddenly stopped kissing me and gasped. I quickly turned around to see the hurt, confused look on his face as he stared at the blood that was on his hand. I reached up and rubbed the spot where he was kissing me to feel the wet, warmth of blood dripping from one of the welts the extension cord my mother had used to beat us had left behind. I quickly wiped the blood off of my hand on to my dingy black uniform pants before zipping up my jacket and trying to brush off the situation.

"Oh that was just an insect bite that I scratched and it turned into a sore. It's okay though." I said to Jerrod as he continued to just stand there staring at me with his bloody hand in the air.

I could tell that he wasn't believing anything I said as I tried to force a smile and he just continued to stand there. After about a second of awkwardness, I turned around to walk away as Jerrod stepped forward and grabbed my arm. He turned me around and grabbed my face in his hands as he used his thumbs to wipe away small patches of the make-up on my cheeks. When he saw the bruises and cuts that were under the pound of liquid foundation and concealer I had on, I watched Jerrod's sorrow turn into deep concern and anger.

"Who did this to you, Tisha? Who did it, yo mama? Maine, what the fuck? Why did she do this to you? Baby, I'm so sorry. Please Tisha, come home with me today. I will protect you. You can stay with me at my brother's house as long as you want to. You can bring your brother and sister too, whatever you need just please baby don't go back there. Let me help you." Jerrod said as he pleaded with me using his eyes and his words.

I felt tears roll down my cheeks as he kissed me on my forehead and pulled me close to him. I wanted nothing more than to be with him and finally be worry-free, not having to wonder if I will be beaten, raped, or sold at any time. I knew that Jerrod would protect me as much as he could, but I also knew he had his own demons. I knew that his brother was just as possessive and angry when he drank as his father was. I also knew that he didn't really want Jerrod living with him, but he agreed just to get the monthly stipend their mother provided. With issues of his own at home, I did not want to ruin the love we had just found by complicating his life even more.

"No baby, it's okay. She'll be okay today. It's Friday and she gets checks from Shamel's dad on Fridays. She won't let him see Sha and pretends he is a deadbeat dad, but every Friday her $350 check is there waiting on her and by Sunday morning she's broke and there's no food in the house." I said to Jerrod without realizing it until it was too late.

That happened a lot when I was around him. He made me feel so comfortable and safe that I would let my guard down and just let my true feelings and emotions out.

"Well, I got some money if you need it. As a matter of fact, here." Jerrod said taking a wad of cash out of his pocket and peeling off two, crisp one hundred dollar bills and handing them to me.

I shook my head and tried to protest as I handed the money back to him. I couldn't take his money. Although, I knew that two hundred dollars would go a long way, I didn't want to take his money because I didn't want to seem like anyone's charity case. Jerrod pushed the money back into my palm as he smiled at me and put his arm over my shoulder, totally disregarding my resistance.

"You can go ahead and put that in your pocket, Tisha, because I'm not taking it back. And before you think it, I didn't give it to you because I feel sorry for you or no shit like that. I gave it to you because I love you and a man is supposed to take care of his woman. Besides, I don't feel sorry for you anyway. If anything, I admire you because not many females can go through the shit you go through every day and still come to school, get good grades, and do it all with a smile on their faces. And aside from that be thick and beautiful as hell...Owww, you a bad girl, Tisha Lewis!" Jerrod said jokingly as the sad, pained look on my face turned into a big, bright smile.

Jerrod made me feel so good that I forgot all about the bruises all over my face and the pain in my body as we talked and walked hand-in-hand to school. Inside the building, we were greeted by stares, whispers, and a lot people speaking to us. It was like I had turned into an instant celebrity as the girls, who always made fun of me or simply ignored me, began to speak and ask me questions. The rest of the morning I breezed through my classes with ease, pleasantly surprised with the new calm, welcoming atmosphere me whooping Roxxy's ass had created.

At lunch Jerrod sat with me and ordered us every item on the lunch menu they had for sale in the cafeteria. I noticed all eyes were on us as Jerrod fed me fries and leaned over every once in a while to kiss me on my neck. I saw envy in the eyes of some of the girls who liked him as I glanced around the room, loving the attention I was finally getting, good and bad. Although most of the senior girls who liked Jerrod rolled their eyes and whispered behind my back, I knew that no one would dare say anything to me to my face in fear that I would go crazy like I had done on Roxxy.

By the time the school day was over, I walked out of the building happy, and for once in my life feeling like I mattered as Jerrod held my hand and we went into the Overlook. After sitting around with the guys in the trap and watching Jerrod play Call of Duty with Buddy for a while, Terricka finally appeared with her money and we prepared to leave. I kissed Jerrod long and passionately at the door before he asked me again to come and stay with him and I declined.

"Remember that the offer is always open, baby. Call me if you need me, Tisha." Jerrod whispered before kissing me again.

I stood there in the doorway for a minute still lingering in Jerrod Jordan's cologne feeling his soft lips on mine. I didn't want to leave him, but I knew I had to. I reluctantly walked away, looking back at Jerrod every second as he blew kisses at me and Terricka laughed while pulling my arm. The entire walk to the Boys & Girls Club to get Sha all I could think about was Jerrod and how good he made me feel. I was in a love haze as Terricka left me to go in and get Sha. While she was gone, I sat on the curb reliving my time with Jerrod. I was so wrapped up in my daydream I didn't even notice Sha and Terricka had come out of the building until Sha kissed me on the forehead, startling me back into reality.

"Thinking about ya boo, huh? Tisha and Jerrod, sitting in the tree. K-I-S-S-I-N-G!" Sha sang as I got up and chased him down the street giggling with Terricka following us.

We laughed and played all the way to Wendy's on Thomas before sitting down and having a great meal. After we ate, we all walked home in silence, anticipating the mayhem that would unfold. I don't know why, but it was like we could feel tragedy before it struck. Somehow we knew that something bad was about to happen when we got home, but there was nothing we could do to stop it. All we could do was hope that the storm wouldn't be too bad or last for a long time. I prayed that God would shield and protect us from all pain and harm as we walked up to our building and noticed all of the lights upstairs were on.

"Lord just give me strength. Protect us from whatever madness lies behind this door." I said out loud before opening the door and walking in.

Chapter 7

Terricka and Sha trailed behind me as I opened the door and my hands trembled while turning the knob. I held my breath as the door made its usual squeaky sound, alerting my mother that someone was coming in. I hated that snitch ass door because if you didn't open it just right it would sound the alarm and my mother would come running like a lion ready to pounce just to see who it was. She didn't come running that time though. I paused once inside the living room, waiting for her to come down the steps yelling and cursing. However, I didn't hear or see her anywhere. All I saw was an immaculate living room, void of all drug baggies, garbage, and the usual, stale, musky, crack smell that lingered in the air.

To our surprise someone had cleaned up the house from top to bottom and even did the laundry, which was stacked up neatly in separate piles on the table by the front door. Sha looked at me in disbelief as Terricka pushed me to the side to look around the rest of the downstairs. All I could do was stare at the bright yellow walls, which I swore were brown due to the dirt buildup that had been on them all of my life. I couldn't figure out what was going on as I walked over to the couch and ran my fingers over the cool, damp fabric. Someone had even cleaned the upholstery on the tattered, second-hand couch, loveseat and chair we had in the living room.

"What the hell is going on? I know she not….It couldn't be." I said to myself out loud as I racked my brain trying to figure out what was going on.

The last time my mother had cleaned or did anything beneficial to us was when she went back on her meds for a day to receive her child support back pay from Shamel's father. That was over two years ago and it only lasted 24 hours because as soon as the meds wore off my mother was back to her usual mean, insane self. She spent the entire day breaking and destroying everything beautiful she had done when she was on her meds. Her down periods after taking meds were much worse than her usual insane fits and I hoped like hell she was not about to repeat that cycle again.

"What the fuck? Tisha, Sha... come here." Terricka said from the kitchen, startling me out of my thoughts as Sha and I ran to see what was going on.

When I ran into the kitchen I knew right then that my worst nightmare was indeed true. The usually dirty, stinky kitchen Terricka and I worked to clean each day was absolutely spotless without a dish in the sink. Sha quickly opened the refrigerator to reveal that it was filled with fruits, veggies, milk, and eggs, and there was actually name brand cereal in the cabinets. I watched my brother's eyes light up as he quickly went over to the cabinet and got him out a dish to make a bowl of Fruit Loops.

I could do nothing but stand there and wonder as I watched Terricka's facial expression go from a look of confusion to one of suspicion. I could tell that she was trying to figure out what was going on just like I was as she looked at me out of the side of her eye. I nodded my head at my sister, letting her know that we were sharing thoughts as she continued to stare at me.

"I don't trust this shit either, T." I said to my sister as I went over to the refrigerator to snatch down the picture of my mother, Sha, Terricka, and

I back when Sha was five years old and we went to the fair.

That was one of my fondest memories of my mother when she was on her meds and had her shit together. I used to love to see that picture and relive our happier days. However, after being beaten, sold, and treated like a dog for so long, I didn't have hope of getting those happy times back. I didn't want to see those fairytale pictures, reminding me of a happier time I would never get back. All I wanted was to finally get away from the hell living I had to endure with my mother and never return.

"We gotta find Denise, Tisha. We gotta find her and see what's going on. You know how this scenario plays out and I'm not going through that bullshit again." Terricka said to me as she walked out of the kitchen and I followed.

We left Sha in the kitchen eating his cereal, oblivious to the shit storm that was brewing as we went upstairs to find our mother. Terricka led the way, breathing hard and clenching her fists as I walked behind her holding my breath and anticipating the worst. When we got on the landing, I looked towards my mother's room and I could hear her humming a church song under her breath. I looked at Terricka in astonishment at the same time as she looked at me, totally dumbfounded.

"Is that mama singing? What's going on, Tisha?" Terricka asked me as my mother suddenly appeared in the hallway.

When she stepped out on to the landing, I felt the breath in my body leave. I couldn't believe my eyes as my mother walked towards us with a blue sweater dress and knee high boots on. Her hair was clean and neatly curled, she had on makeup, and her eyes were as clear as I had ever saw them. I knew right then that it was true that my mother was back on her meds and for a brief moment sane. The only question that kept nagging me was why she was back on her meds? I didn't have to wonder about that long as my mother came over and hugged me and Terricka before she spoke.

"Hey my babies, my Tisha and Terricka. I'm so glad y'all are home. Mommy is about to finish dinner and then we have a meeting with the social worker to ensure Shamel keeps getting his support. Maybe when the meeting is over, we can all have movie night. What do you think ladies? By the way, where is Shamel?" My mother asked us as Terricka and I looked at her like she had lost her damn mind.

It was crazy to me how my mother could be the perfect woman when she was on her meds and the most evil devil from hell when she wasn't. It was that wishy-washy demeanor that made me not trust my mother at all.

"Sha downstairs. Ma, are you back on your meds and if so for how long this time? Will we wake up in the morning to the crazy Denise again or will we smell fresh muffins and Pine Sol when we open our eyes? Well, which one is it mother because I'm tired of this shit. One day you love us and the next day you hate us, we're tired of it Denise." Terricka said with tears streaming down her cheeks as she rolled her eyes and smacked her lips.

My mother tried to grab my sister and pull her into an embrace, but Terricka pushed her away before turning back to me.

"I am not about to go through this bullshit with Denise. You can stay here and play like the Huxtables if you want to, but I'm out of here. I'm not about to pretend with her crazy ass. I'll be back tonight when this bullshit is over." Terricka said to me before rolling her eyes at our mother and stomping down the steps.

I watched my sister disappear down the stairs before turning back around to face my mother, who was staring down the steps with tears in her eyes. The sad look on my mother's face when I looked at her almost made me forget all of the horrible things she had done to me. It seemed that no matter how much she hurt me and told me she hated me, I still loved her deep down, and didn't want to see her hurting. Against my better judgment, I reached over and wiped away the tears streaming down my mother's cheeks as her frown quickly turned into a smile.

For that split second in time, I could feel my mother's love as we gazed into each other's eyes. Seeing my mother in her right mind and actually expressing an emotion other than anger touched my heart for a moment. Gone were the 'I hate you's' and I wish she would just die. In that moment, I was a little girl again and my mother was loving me like only she could. I wanted that moment to last forever. My heart told me to have hope that things would be different and I tried to hold on to that glimmer of hope, even though my mind told me not to.

"It's okay, mama. I know it hurts to see Terricka so mad, but you have to understand this is all your fault. You have done some horrible things, mama, and we will probably never be able to forgive you for them. But, none of that matters right now though. All that matters is keeping you on your meds, happy, and being a real mama. So if that means I have to pretend for the authorities, so be it. Sha deserves some time with the real you." I said to my mother as she sniffled while hugging me and then turn to walk away.

I watched her as she went back into her room and turned the vacuum on to finish cleaning. I sighed at the thought of her new responsible mother act being just a ploy to keep her check as I went into me and Terricka's room. Inside I found that my mother had cleaned that as well. All of our clothes were neatly folded and hung up and there was new outfits and shoes for us laying on the bed.

I walked over to the bed and sat down, running my fingers over the soft, pink, cotton sweater and black skirt that my mother had set out for me. I couldn't help but to get choked up as I admired the accessories and brand new panty and bra set that was also laid out.

It was apparent to me that my mother had put great thought into the items she bought us, I just couldn't understand why she wouldn't do that all of the time. Why couldn't she be the mother she was supposed to be when it mattered the most? When no one was watching? I couldn't figure out why her love and compassion always had to come at an astronomical cost. As I listened to my mother sing and clean like a Stepford Wife, I was sure that I wasn't going to figure out the answers to any of my questions before the meds wore off and she transformed back into a demon. That's why instead of dwelling on the inevitable, I got up off my ass, grabbed my clothes, and went into the bathroom to shower and get dressed. I decided that I was going to reap some of the benefits of having a sane mother before it all came to an end.

After my hot shower in the newly cleaned bathroom, I went downstairs feeling refreshed and renewed. Sha was in front of the TV watching afternoon cartoons when I entered. I couldn't help but to smile as I watched him lying on the freshly shampooed carpet, eating a bag of chips, smacking away like he didn't have a care in the world. I loved to see him so happy and out of his shell. I rarely had the opportunity to watch him enjoy being at home so that sight really warmed my heart.

"You enjoying yourself, huh Twerp?" I said to Sha as he giggled and I bent down to steal one of his chips on my way to the kitchen.

Like Sha, I was not going to waste time being mad or wondering how long the happiness would last. Instead I was going to take advantage of what I had right then. When I walked around the corner to the kitchen, the smell of lasagna, pork chops, and fresh garlic bread hit my nose at once. My stomach churned as I stood in the doorway and watched my mother take the lasagna and garlic bread out of the oven before turning to look at me.

"Ahhh, my Tisha. I knew you were coming down when the aroma hit your nose. See, mama made your favorite foods. Everything gonna be alright, baby. And you look so beautiful in your new outfit...I wish Terricka was here. But, I won't spoil the moment with ugliness, we all must be on our best behavior today. Now, go set the table for me, please." My mother said to me while winking her eye and wearing a huge smile on her face.

Even though she had hurt me to my core on numerous occasions, I couldn't deny the happiness I felt seeing her well again. Somewhere deep inside of me a seedling of hope sprouted as I smiled back at my mother before walking over to the new dining room table and setting three places.

"No baby, set four places. Mrs. Jenkins, Sha's social worker, is having dinner with us. AND I WANT BOTH YOU AND SHA ON YOUR BEST BEHAVIOR. YOU HEAR ME, SHAMEL?" My mother yelled into the living room with a big, fake smile on her face as she stepped into the doorway to stare my brother down.

Right then, I remembered why I couldn't stand my mother and why I didn't trust her. I didn't like her or trust her because I knew that she would never change. I was so happy to have her back with us, I had ignored the voice in my head that told me she was acting. However, beneath the surface, I knew that she was sober and on her meds for one reason, and one reason only, to get the check. Everything she was doing was just a part of her master plan. There was no real love or genuine praise there, only the med induced emotions and unrelenting tricks of a junky wrapped up in a clean, pretty little package. My mother was showing her true colors before the meds had even wore off, yet I still obeyed.

"Yes mama." I said as I finished setting the table and walked towards the living room.

I stopped and stood in the doorway, watching my mother place the lasagna, pork chops, and garlic bread in the middle of the table before standing back to admire her work. She looked so proud as she straightened the napkin in the basket holding the pork chops. I shook my head as I walked out of the kitchen still trying to decide how I felt about what was happening. As soon as I sat down on the couch and grabbed the remote control, someone knocked on the door and my mother came running like a track star.

I hadn't seen my mother move that fast since the dope man gave out free samples. She came to an abrupt stop in front of the door as she quickly turned her body towards Sha and me before leaning in to whisper.

"Now remember what I said both of you. We are going to have a pleasant dinner. Only speak when spoken to and be short. Say what we have rehearsed a million times and then it will all be over. When it's done, we'll have movie night. Now smile babies, mommy loves you!" My mother said changing her emotions six different times as she spoke.

Sha and I looked at one another and then turned to look at our mother open the door for Mrs. Jenkins with the biggest, fakest smile we had ever seen on her face. Everything about our mother was fake and seemed rehearsed as she complimented the tall, slender, dark skinned, frumpy lady in a teal pants suit, on how lovely she looked. I almost snickered when I heard that bullshit and saw that the stupid social worker was actually buying it. It just amazed me that such dumb, incompetent people where in such an important position as ensuring the safety of children.

That explained why we never got help though. I guess it didn't dawn on the social worker that she should have actually investigated to do her job effectively. A little observing would have surely raised her suspicion if she had sense after all of the allegations and police calls to our house. However, it seemed she paid no attention to any of that nor the reason why she was doing home visits in the first place. Shamel's father wasn't just concerned with his safety for nothing. He had petitioned the court for custody or at the least visits a dozen times, but was denied because of the domestic violence charge he got trying to take us from our mother.

Shamel's father Shaheim's past and desire to help us had caused him his freedom and his rights to be a good father to his child while my crazy, drug addicted mother continued her reign of terror right under their noses. Thinking about how I watched Shaheim cry and call Shamel's name the day he was arrested trying to take us away from the wild party our mother was having at home, made me angry again. I was going to go along with my mother's game, but I wouldn't pretend to enjoy it. Fuck that. If she was going to act, so was I.

When we sat down to eat dinner, I remained quiet, keeping my head down and answering every question with nasty, rude, one word answers. By the time my mother served her gross, sticky rice pudding, Mrs. Jenkins seemed to be at the end of her rope with my attitude. I expected her to question my mother about what was going on with my behavior or ask me why I was acting out. However, that stupid, stick of a woman simply complimented my mother on recovering successfully and handling a difficult teenager on her own.

Before I could catch myself, I grunted loudly and got up to excuse myself to my room. I heard Shamel get up and follow me towards the steps, but I didn't look back. I didn't want to look at my mother with her fake ass as she told Mrs. Jenkins it was just hormones and I would be okay. I wanted to yell out that it wasn't my fucking hormones it was my heart crying out for help, but I just kept walking instead. When we got upstairs, I heard my mother slam the front door and laugh about her stellar performance. I quickly pushed Sha into my room and slammed the door, knowing what I had just done and that the social worker was gone.

Sha sat on the end of the bed and watched me with wide eyes as I slid the dresser in front of the door. Seconds later I had my ear pressed up against the peeling, cracked wood as I listened for my mother. I could hear her footsteps as she ran up the stairs. My heart raced and my legs trembled as I heard my mother stop in front of my door. I pushed the dresser against the door and closed my eyes, wishing I could just rewind time. I wished I could take everything back or simply erase the moment I was conceived. In my heart I think that if I could have, I would have made sure my father's sperm never met that egg. However, I couldn't do any of those things. All that I could do was hold my breath and wait for it to be over.

After a few minutes, I could hear my mother walk passed my door slowly and go into her room for a second. I just stood there taking short, shallow breaths with the dresser wedged between my body and the door as I listened to my mother walk around her room, come out on to the landing, and then run back down stairs. I was finally able to relax my tense muscles and breathe again after I heard the front door slam and lock. I sighed in relief when Sha came over and hugged me as he cried into my chest.

"Why she act like that, Tisha? Why can't she be normal and stay like that? When are we gonna have a real life, huh?" My brother asked me as he looked up at me with tear filled eyes.

I wanted so badly to tell him that everything would be okay and that happy endings were possible for people like us. I wanted to ease his pain and fears and promise him a bright future, but I couldn't. I couldn't because at that moment I couldn't see our lives getting any better. All I could see was things getting progressively worse and then ending with me having to make the hardest decision of my life. I didn't see the pot of gold at the end of the rainbow. All I saw was more hurt on top of pain, but like the daughter of a true actress I was able to put on a brave face for Sha.

"Everything is gonna work out little brother. Everything in life happens for a reason and although we may not understand it at the time, God never makes mistakes. He is just testing us now to make sure we are ready for our blessings. Just stay strong little brother. I love you, now go in your room, barricade the door, and go to sleep." I said to Sha as he smiled at me and I kissed him gently on the forehead.

I watched my brother go into his room and listened to him slide his dresser in front of the door before I returned to mine. Inside I laid in the bed staring at the ceiling going over the events of the day. Anger tried to consume me as I remembered my mother and her fakeness at dinner, spinning a web of lies just to keep a check. Tears ran down my cheeks as I envisioned her face with that big, fake ass smile.

I sat up in the bed and took deep breaths, trying to regain my composure as jolts of rage surged through me.

"Calm down, Tisha. She's not worth your anger. Think about Jerrod…think about his love." I said to myself as I envisioned Jerrod's sexy, dark chocolate skin, deep dimples, and beautiful hazel eyes.

In no time my breathing returned to normal and I felt my body relax as I laid back in my bed. The last thing I remembered was imagining Jerrod's face and feeling his lips pressed against mine as we kissed in the hallway at school.

The next thing I knew I was being yanked down to the foot of the bed by my ankles and someone was pulling off my gown. I opened my eyes and tried to focus on the figure hovering over me as the bright light beamed down hurting my eyes. I squinted and used my hand to block the light as I tried to adjust my eyes to see. When my vision finally came into focus, I almost died as I looked into the face of destruction.

Chapter 8

Suddenly Jerome's big, ashy lips were over my mouth and part of my nose making it difficult to breathe as I pulled my knees up into his chest and tried to peel the fucking skin off of his face with my nails. I couldn't believe what was happening as I continued to fight Jerome and he continued to put his stinky, cigarette smelling tongue all down my throat. I felt vomit rise up into my esophagus as Jerome touched my uvula with his tongue and moaned out my name.

"Ummmm, Tisha, I finally caught you alone, huh? Too bad I'm not alone...so let's get this *ménage a trios* started." Jerome said as my heart beat a mile a minute and someone suddenly grabbed my arms pulling them over my head as Jerome buried his face in my vagina.

I looked up to see the upside down face of a man about thirty years old with a fat stomach and huge lips. He had on a dirty wife beater and gray, dingy jogging pants that had a huge hole in the crotch. He smiled at me and licked his lips as I screamed and yelled while trying to squeeze Jerome's brains out with my inner thighs.

"LET ME GOOOOOO! DENISE, WHERE THE FUCK ARE YOU? HOW COULD YOU DO THIS TO ME, YOU BITCH? I DID WHAT YOU SAID, STOP THEM PLEASSSEEE! TERRICKA, HELP ME!!" I screamed and cried as Jerome came up from licking on me with a huge smile on his face, smacking the insides of my legs so hard he left his hand print behind.

I yelled out in pain and tried to kick again as I glared at Jerome with hate. He laughed before putting his knees on my ankles to pin my legs down as he went in his pocket and got a rubber out to slip it on. I spit and cursed at him as he took his penis out, put the condom on, and licked his tongue out at me.

"What the fuck I tell you last time, princess? You doing all this fighting when I'm gonna get it anyway. Now be a good little hoe like yo mama, or else." Jerome said as he laid his fat, stinky body on top of mine and told the man to let my wrists go.

As soon as he let go of my hands, I went crazy punching and kicking Jerome as hard as I could, trying to get him off of me; however, there was no use. My little licks had no effect on the massive beast who was having his way with me. If anything, it just annoyed him and in a sick ass way turned him on. He quickly smacked me across the face as I continued to scream and fight. The impact from the slap with his big, rusty hand was so hard my ears began to ring as my teeth chattered. I was so discombobulated that I couldn't do anything as he flipped me on top of him in the bed and the other man snatched my gown off, throwing it on the floor.

Jerome entered me rough and hard, causing me to let out a blood curdling scream as I fought and he held me tightly around the waist. Pain and rage surged through my body as I did all I could to get away from the monster holding me. As I continued to fight, Jerome and he laughed. I could suddenly feel the other man's hands on the back of my thighs as he ran his fingers up my leg to my ass. I squirmed and tried to knock his hands off of my ass as Jerome continued to thrust inside of me and tears ran down my cheeks. I was trying as hard as I could and praying to God for help, but it seemed no one heard my cries.

For a second, I just gave up as Jerome moved me up and down on top of him and licked on my breasts while the other man put his entire face in my ass. That was the worst moment of my life as I laid there defeated, motionless being violated in ways no human, let alone a child, should ever experience. I felt a piece of me die that second as the man who was licking my ass licked all the way up to my ear before kissing and licking my neck. I gagged and dry heaved as the shitty smell of his breath hit my nose and he grabbed the back of my hair to pull my head back.

"Little bitch, you in no position to act siddity. I paid good money so I expect a good nut, now act like the good little hoe I heard you are. I got 10 inches of hard dick I know you will like." The stanky, foul mouth bastard on my back said, holding my hair as he licked my neck again before ramming his penis into my anus.

The pain I experienced that second was like no other pain I had ever felt. Suddenly, my eyebrows were burning, I couldn't breathe, and every muscle in my body was stiff. I felt like I died at that second as he ripped open the one hole on the human body never intended to be an entrance and proceeded to thrust and gyrate his hips. I gasped and clawed at Jerome's eyes as the man on my back slowly slid himself deeper inside of me and Jerome squeezed my waist as he pumped faster.

My head began to spin and I think I blacked out or went into a trance for a second because the next thing I knew Jerome was screaming out in pain. I suddenly broke out of his embrace and planted my knee right in his nuts as I punched and clawed at his eyes. My quick actions knocked the man on my ass to the floor as Jerome continued to scream and I tried to get up to run. When I lifted up on my knees, they felt weak and there was excruciating pain in my ass and the top of my thighs.

I could feel the warm blood running down the back of my legs as I put one foot on the floor and prepared to get the fuck away. The only problem was before I could even put my other shaking, weak leg on the bed, Jerome sat up and punched me in the stomach so hard vomit spewed out of my mouth all on the wall and floor. I fell forward on the bed gasping for air as pain shot up through my stomach to the top of my head. It felt like Jerome had broken every bone in my body with that punch because I could feel it rattle in my soul. In seconds Jerome was up on his knees in the bed, pinning me down to the bed by my neck as he punched me in my side and back.

"Bitch have you lost yo fucking mind. You little bitches have no manners, so I guess I gotta teach you the same way I teach Roxxy when she don't wonna please daddy! Stupid Little bitch!" Jerome yelled into my ear as he punched me over and over again as I gasped for air.

I thought he was going to beat me to death as I squirmed under his grip, getting the worse of the punches he was throwing in my arms as I blocked. After a couple of more punches, the pain became unbearable and I passed out, falling limp on top of Jerome.

When I opened my eyes, I almost forgot where I was at until I felt the pressure of someone's hand around the back of my neck pinning me to the bed as they thrust inside of me from behind. I squirmed and tried to scream as Jerome moaned and the man with him yelled out his name.

"JEROME…nigga, I'm outta here. I didn't sign up for beating and fucking unconscious young hoes. Nigga, you gone go to jail by yo muthafucking self." The man said as he left out of the room leaving the door open.

I screamed and stretched my neck as far as I could to see into the hall once the man left. When I was finally able to see outside the room, I could do nothing but scream as I watched my mother walk passed the door smoking a cigarette and smiling at me before going down the steps and leaving the house. I felt my heart stop when I heard her slam the door behind her so hard that the windows shook. My body began to shiver and I cried from my soul as I learned that love really didn't love nobody, especially not me. My mother had tricked me into showing her love again, and in return she spit in my face. My heart was broken as I laid there beneath a woolly mammoth sobbing.

"Aww lil Tisha, it's gonna be okay." Jerome whispered into my ear laughing as he continued to thrust deep and hard inside of me from behind.

"It's okay because I gotcha. Don't nobody want you or care about you but me. You my lil hoe now. I gotcha since nobody else does." Jerome said laughing as he stuck his tongue in my ear and thrust inside of me.

I closed my eyes as tears ran across my face, ready to give up and just face my fate as a hoe. I was ready to be defeated and let every nasty thing people in the hood had ever said about me come true. I was on the verge of just jumping into the dark side and letting go until I heard the words of our Salvation Song in my mind, telling me to hold on. I could hear my sister singing the lyrics too and willing me to hold on because she was on her way. All of my pain seemed to disappear in that moment as I opened my mouth and began singing the lyrics to the song, throwing Jerome off.

"Nothing is forever what we're hoping for,
No more pain so don't you cry anymore.
Hold your head up high and dry yo tears,
Let me help you through and erase yo fears.
We'll overcome it all if we stick together,
We just gotta believe nothing lasts forever (nothing lasts forever)."
I sang from my heart as tears streamed down my face.

Suddenly, as I continued to sing and Jerome was frozen on top of me just staring into my face, I got a glimpse of my sister as she slipped into the room behind Jerome. She was holding the same metal bat my mother broke her hand with. I held my breath as I watched my sister raise the bat up high over her head and knock the fuck out of Jerome's nasty, rapist, pedophile ass. The impact from the blow with the bat was so loud when it hit Jerome's skull it sounded like a basketball hitting concrete.

Jerome fell off of me and on to the floor immediately as Terricka dropped the bat and rushed over to help me up to my feet. I felt a little more strength and was able to move my legs better as I stood up and grabbed my gown to put it back on. Terricka helped me pull it over my head and as soon as it was down, covering my body and I could see, I realized we had fucked up. Jerome was up on his feet standing right behind Terricka with the ugliest look I had ever seen on his face. He grabbed Terricka by the back of her neck with both hands, lifting her up off her feet as I screamed and ran over to the bed.

I reached under the mattress searching for the knife my uncle Scooby gave me as I watched my sister squirm in the air and claw at Jerome's hands as her eyes rolled in the back of her head. I found the knife in seconds and quickly flicked it open like my uncle taught me before lunging at Jerome and sticking him in the left side of his lower stomach. I stuck the knife in as hard and deep as I could, causing him to drop my sister and grab his abdomen. Terricka got up on her feet and ran over to me as we stood there frozen for a few minutes while Jerome yelled and growled as he pulled the knife out, throwing it on the floor. We screamed and ran for the door just as he grabbed Terricka in the back of her hair slanging her to the floor.

Jerome was like a wild animal as he slung my sister around the room and I jumped on his back. He drug Terricka over to the wall as he turned around to pin me against it using his body. I felt out of breath from his massive weight against my little petite body and welcomed the relief that came when he finally walked away, leaving me to slide down the wall. I laid there out of breath for a second as Jerome carried my sister over to the bed and began pulling her clothes off as she fought him. I gathered my strength and jumped on his back screaming, only to have him flip me over his head on to the bed, pushing Terricka to the side as he straddled me. He put both of his hands around my neck and squeezed as I felt my eyes bulge out of my head and spit run from my mouth.

Just as everything began to get blurry and I was about to lose consciousness, I felt Jerome suddenly stop moving. I watched as his eyes popped out of his head and he opened his mouth but no words came out. I looked around him and saw my sister standing there behind him with the knife in her hand as she stabbed him over and over again, fast and with precision. After about four good stabs, Jerome released my neck and stood up with his arms out, wobbling from side-to-side. My sister remained beside him wherever he went, grunting as she held the knife in his gut. Terricka screamed and yelled telling Jerome how much she hated him as she twisted the knife in the wound. He yelled out in anguish as my sister let go of the knife and I ran over to her before we both burst out of the door. On the landing, we both stood frozen contemplating what we should do.

"We gotta go get Sha." I said to Terricka just as we heard our mother come into the door downstairs, talking loud and laughing.

We both knew that the meds had completely wore off and that our mother was back to her old ways again. That meant that it wouldn't end well for us when she saw what we had done. Terricka and I turned around to run to Sha's room just as he opened his door and motioned for us to hurry up. As we ran passed our open bedroom door, I got a glimpse of Jerome dragging himself to the door, leaking all over the place. I knew that it would only be a few minutes before he got to the top of the steps and called for help. That meant my sister and I had to move fast.

Terricka and I hurried into Sha's room before he slammed the door and locked it, pushing his dresser back in front of it. I went straight over to the second floor window and opened it wide before turning around to face my brother and sister. Terricka nodded her head yes and pushed Sha forward as he shook his head no and resisted. Sha was scared of heights and at that second I knew it would be impossible to get him to go out of the window, slide down the side of the roof, and then jump off. Even if it wasn't that high, I knew my brother would never do it.

"I can't do that, Tisha, y'all just go without me. It's y'all that they want not me. I'm just gonna hide until he police come and then I'll go to social services. At least I'll be safe for tonight and y'all will too. Now get out of here. I love you, Tisha… I love you, Terricka." My little brother said through his tears as we both ran over to hug and kiss him.

Before we could finish our heartfelt, emotional moment, the shrill cry of a wounded Jerome filled our ears. Sha pushed us towards the window as we heard our mother and the other people downstairs yell up to Jerome asking what happened. We didn't wait to see what his response would be because before I knew it, Terricka and I had both climbed out of the window and slid down the side of the roof in our flimsy clothing. I still had on the thin, ripped pink, cotton gown I wore to sleep with nothing underneath it and my sister only had on her white t-shirt and black panties after Jerome had ripped her pants off.

Terricka and I were both almost naked when we jumped off that roof and into the bushes in front of our apartment. We didn't give a fuck about that though. We had tried an escape from prison and successfully pulled it off, that's all that mattered. We timed our jump just right too as we both landed on our feet and kept running. I could hear the boys across the mall from us yelling and asking us what was wrong as we sped around the building towards Lisa'a house. Their questions were followed by the sound of my mother screaming our name and saying that she was calling the police on us. Her threats didn't matter much to us at that moment because all we wanted to do was get the fuck away.

By the time we made it to Lisa's building, both Terricka and I were out of breath and our bodies shook from the surge of pure adrenaline. I quickly knocked on the door and listened as Lisa and Tank argued loudly on the other side. I looked at Terricka and we both sighed knowing that it was one of those times Tank was whooping Lisa's ass and she wouldn't want us around. After another knock on the door by Terricka, I could her Lisa dragging her feet as she slowly walked to the door snatching it open and pressing her face against the screen of the security door.

The alcohol on her breath hit me with force from several feet away and I quickly realized things weren't about to go as planned. That and the fact that she was still standing there on the other side of the door without opening it while sucking her teeth let me know that something was about to go down.

"Let us in, Lisa, maine for real. Some bad shit just went down. Jerome raped Tisha and I had to stab him. Denise fina call the police on us and lie, we need somewhere to hide. Let us in please." Terricka pleaded with Lisa as she grabbed the handle of the screen door and Lisa shook her head no.

I couldn't believe what was happening as I stood there with tears in my eyes and blood, cuts, and bruises all over my body as Lisa refused to let us in. I couldn't understand why the one person who always showed us loved was turning her back on us when we needed her the most. I couldn't understand it as I stood there looking my godmother in her eyes, but I was about to find out.

"Naw lil mama's, y'all can't come over here and kick it no more. Y'all funky ass mammy fucked my nigga in my house and left her filthy ass panties in my butter dish with a note saying she won. Yeah, she won alright. She won this major ass whooping whenever I see her junky ass. And to top it off this bitch came back and broke in my muthafucking house after my nigga wouldn't let her suck his dick again. That bitch has violated me for the last time and I'm dragging that hoe as soon as I see her. SO, I guess to answer y'all question the answer is HELL NO! I can't hide y'all or fuck with y'all at all no mo. Now get the fuck off of my doorstep!" Lisa yelled before slamming the door in our faces and leaving us standing there.

I couldn't stop the whirlwind of emotions that hit me at that moment when the one person who always had our back walked away because of our mama. Once again the sins of our mother had cost us something we would probably never be able to get back. I was crushed knowing that we had no one left. Our grandma was in Mississippi since our evil aunt Kim had forced her to move away. Lisa was all we had and in an instant she was gone.

"What we gonna do, T? We ain't got nobody. We might as well go turn ourselves the fuck in." I said sobbing as my sister put her arm over my shoulder and pushed me forward.

Tears ran down my face as we made our way out of our apartments and the early morning sky lit up with lightning strikes. It was 3 a.m. in mid-February, yet it was usually warm that night as we walked with no coats, pants, or shoes on without being cold. We walked in silence with nothing but our sniffles and the thunder raging around us echoing in our ears until the rain began to pour down. I looked up at the sky directly into the rain clouds and asked the Lord to send us some help. I hoped that some way, our curse would be lifted for a second and everything wouldn't end in tragedy for us like it always did.

Just as Terricka and I crossed the street and walked into the parking lot of the North Gate shopping center, God answered my prayers. A blue Crown Victoria whipped up in front of us fast, cutting us off and causing us to stop dead in our tracks. I stood there in my wet, transparent nightgown, holding my sister's hand as we waited for the next round of devastation to hit. Instead though, it seemed as if the clouds disappeared and the sun shone only on us as Jerrod jumped out of the car and swooped me up in his arms as he yelled for his brother to help Terricka. I looked up into the face of the love of my life as rain poured down on us and he cried.

"I got you, Tisha, I love you baby and I'll never let anyone hurt you again." Were the last words I heard Jerrod say before the stress of the day took over and I blacked out.

Chapter 9

I woke up the next morning so the sound of
a woman humming as she dabbed a strong liquid
on my skin. I batted my eyes, opening and closing
them trying to get them to focus. When my vision
finally became clear, I looked up into the beautiful,
bruised face of a cocoa colored woman with big
hazel eyes, deep dimples just like Jerrod's, and a
pair of small, black cat woman glasses with
diamonds on them. She smiled at me warmly and
encouraged me to remain laying down as I tried to
sit up in the bed but my entire body ached.

"No baby just stay right here, I'm taking
care of you." The woman said as I looked at her
with confusion on my face and she started to
explain.

"I am Jerrod's mother, Amy, and I am a
nurse. Jerrod called me at about 4:30 this morning,
telling me that his friend needed help. When I got
here an hour ago, you were unconscious and in bad
shape. Fortunately, you don't have any broken
bones, just a lot of cuts and bruises. I suspect you
may have a concussion also which is why I urge

you to go to the hospital." Jerrod's mother said as my heart started racing and I protested.

I couldn't let her take me to the hospital and they would call my mother. That would mean the police would show up and Terricka and I would go to juvie. I couldn't risk that.

"Noooo, no hospital. I'm fine. Thank you Mrs. Hill, I appreciate everything you have done for me, but I have to go." I said as I sat up on the bed and my head began to spin and my side ached.

All of the punches I had taken along with the gang rape, had more of a physical and emotional strain on me than I thought as my body shut down on its own and I fell back on to the bed. Jerrod's mother was at my side instantly, wringing out the rag she had in a bowl on the floor and rubbing my forehead with it.

"JERROD.... JERROD. Keith go get Jerrod and tell him to come here now!" Amy yelled to Jerrod's brother who had appeared in the doorway when she was calling Jerrod's name.

My whole body ached as I laid there with my hand laced in Jerrod mother's hand and she told me everything would be okay. I closed my eyes and let exhaustion take me as Jerrod's mother rubbed my head gently like only a real mother would. In seconds I was out like a light only to wake up seconds later to the sounds of Jerrod's mother whispering to him.

"Baby, I can tell you like this girl a lot and I must admit that I already like her too, but you have to be careful dealing with girls who show up all beat up and sexually abused." Jerrod's mother whispered to him as he groaned in agony.

I opened my eyes and tilted my head slightly towards their voices when I heard Jerrod and his mother walk away. I gazed at Jerrod standing there in distress with his hands on his head as his mother told him I had been raped vaginally and anally. Tears streamed down his cheeks as he looked my way and I closed my eyes to pretend like I was still sleep. I could hear him huff and puff and pace the floor as his mother tried to console him. I opened my eyes to see Jerrod punch a hole in the wall by the door before sliding down to the floor. He sat there for a minute with his head in his hands as his mother rubbed his perfectly formed waves.

For a second I thought that me and the baggage that came along with me was too much for Jerrod as he shook his head and said no repeatedly. However, when he suddenly stood up and looked over at me lovingly as I quickly closed my eyes again, I knew that he loved me and would never leave me if he could help it. Although we had only been together a short time, I could feel it in my soul that Jerrod was the one. He was all I ever thought about and even hearing his voice made my heart sing. I prayed for him just as much as I prayed for myself so I knew that what I felt was real love. He was my destiny, that one person God made just for me.

Jerrod dry his tears with his palms and took a deep breath as he turned to talk to his mother.

"I hear what you're saying ma and I respect your opinion. However, just like me or nobody else can tell you to stop loving daddy and leave him alone even although he's an alcoholic that beats you. I feel the same way about Tisha. I know she has her demons, but which one of us don't. I live in a family were I feel inferior and witness violence every day. We both have our crosses to bear living with the sins of our parents. You just told me to think about it and possibly run away because of the bad shit people do to her. I say that's more of a reason to stay. She needs me just like I need her, God made us for each other. Can't you see that? Now, I appreciate your help ma and your words of wisdom, but if you want to be here for me just support me and be there when I need you. I'm your son, but I'm not a little boy anymore. I'm eighteen years old and I have to make my own decisions; good or bad. I want to be with her mama." Jerrod said to his mother in a confident, sincere tone.

I couldn't help but to shed a few tears as I watched Jerrod's mother reach out to hug him as he slowly walked into her arms. A part of me was jealous of their close relationship and seeing Jerrod receive an amount of love from his mother that I would never get from mine. It hurt my heart having to long for a love that was supposed to come naturally.

I closed my eyes and turned my head as I cried for the love I would never have with my mother. I also cried for that little abused girl who had endured so much simply for being born. I cried silently as Jerrod hugged his mother and she told him she would support whatever he did, and when I felt I had all cried out for a hopeless relationship I stopped. I cut off my heart and emotions when it came to my mother and decided I would focus on the love surrounding me and lean on someone who would actually help me up instead of tearing me down. I would focus on loving myself, my siblings, and the one man in my life who showed me real love.

Jerrod walked over to the bed and sat down next to me as I pretended to be sleep. I heard his mother excuse herself from the room followed by the door closing as Jerrod laid down beside me. I felt my heart smile as he gently rubbed my hair before resting his head against mine. I could feel his breath on my neck as he inhaled and exhaled deeply, gathering his thoughts to speak.

"Tisha, I love you, and I promise to always protect you and be there for you no matter what. Know that you never have to hide anything from me, baby…I'll never judge you, and I'm here when you're ready to talk. I will always be here,

Tisha." Jerrod whispered in my ear as tears ran down my face and I turned my head to face him.

He smiled at me with his eyes first and then it gradually spread down the rest of his face. Seeing his emotions come to life before my eyes made the love I felt for Jerrod even more magical. I felt nothing could harm me or make me sad as long as he was around, he wouldn't let it. Jerrod was the best thing I had in my life.

"I love you too, Jerrod, and I never want to leave you." I whispered back to Jerrod as he reached up to wipe away the single, happy tear that rolled down my face before kissing me softly on the lips.

When Jerrod kissed me, I felt sparks of passion all over my body and all of the air left my body. His kiss was like nothing I had felt before. That kiss was 100 times stronger and more passionate than he had kissed me the first day we met. I could feel Jerrod's love as he ran his fingers through my hair before kissing up from my lips to both of my eyes.

"Sleep my queen, mama said you need your rest. When you wake up I'll be right here. You can take a bath and get comfortable and then I'll bring you whatever you want to eat. I'm at your beck and call, baby... I told you I'll take care of you. For real Tisha, I love you. maine!" Jerrod said kissing me on my nose before kissing me deeply on my lips, slipping his tongue in my mouth and caressing my tongue with his.

I kissed Jerrod back flicking my tongue on his as I wrapped my arms around his broad, muscular shoulders. When we released our lip lock, I laid there in his arms as his kissed me in the top of the head and rocked gently from side-to-side. I fell asleep in Jerrod's arms without a care in the world, in love with the thought of being in love. I woke up later that after about 3 o'clock and was greeted by my sister's concerned face. She sat at the edge of the bed with her head down rocking from side-to-side.

"Hey T." I said in a weak hoarse voice as my sister turned around and smiled at me before hugging me tight.

Terricka looked really good like she had a bath and had washed her hair as it laid straight and silky on her shoulders. I smiled at my sister and told her I loved her as she told me how nice Jerrod and his family had been.

"They took care of me like they did you. The lady, Amy fixed up my wounds too. I feel alright so I was about to hit the trap and get some money I just wanted to wait until you were awake. I know Jerrod got you so I don't have to worry. I don't have to worry about Sha either cause I talked to a few people in the hood and they said CPS took him. They said Sha's ass was laughing and skipping to the car when they removed him from the house." My sister said laughing causing me to laugh a little too.

"Oh, they said mama told the police we robbed and stabbed Jerome and he was just over visiting her. They looking for us on robbery and assault with a deadly weapon. She really fucked us off this time. It's okay though because I'm gonna get enough money so we can vanish. Ain't no way you can go back to school now any way. If we get flapped that shit really out of the window. We just gotta go while we can." Terricka said as I sighed thinking about leaving Jerrod behind.

Like when we were kids, Terricka could read my thoughts as she smacked her lips and looked at me sideways.

"Don't tell me you in love with the nigga for real and you don't want to live without him." Terricka said to me laughing as I looked at her with a sincere face.

When I didn't crack a smile, she knew I wasn't playing and quickly changed her position.

"Damn sis, I didn't know you felt like that. It's whatever you want to do. But if we stay here, how you gonna finish school. You would have to be staying for more than just him. Your education is a much better reason." Terricka said as I nodded while thinking of a plan.

I decided I would talk to Mrs. Cunningham and make her believe I needed to be on homebound for medical reasons, then I would complete whatever work I may have at Jerrod's house while I figure out how to handle the law. I would call my mean ass aunt Kim and beg for help if I had to. I just couldn't leave Jerrod. I couldn't.

Terricka agreed to my plan and kissed me before leaving the room. As soon as she let out Jerrod appeared with a beautiful pink Hello kitty pajama set in his hands.

"I got something for you, baby, if you want to shower. Tell me what you want to eat and I'll order it so it can be here by the time you get out." Jerrod said to me as I got up off the bed and walked over to him.

I stood on my tip toes and kissed the tip of Jerrod's nose before taking the clothes off of his arm.

"It doesn't matter to me, baby, whatever you want." I said to Jerrod as we stared at each other intensely until we both burst out in laughter.

It was amazing to me how he could make me happy with no effort. Jerrod kissed me on the forehead before telling me he would order pizza and escorting me to the huge bathroom down the hall. I walked into the beautiful black and white painted bathroom with shiny, black marble floors and chrome fixtures in amazement. I couldn't believe someone like Jerrod's brother Keith could have such good taste and keep a house immaculate. Keith was way too goofy and mean in my eyes to like anything I would like, at least that's what I thought, but I was so wrong.

I peeled off the bloody, crusty gown I had on and stepped into the walk-in shower with the shower head that came down from the ceiling. I fixed the water to a comfortable temperature and let it beam down on me as visions of what happened to me flashed in my mind. I could still see Jerome's beady eyes watching over my body and feel his sloppy lips on my skin. Tears burst forward fast and hard as I continued to see what happened to me. I scrubbed my skin hard and fast with the rag in my hand turning my brown skin red in the places I touched. I sobbed and asked God, 'Why me,' as my body trembled n despair.

Suddenly, I felt the door to the shower open and turned to see Jerod entering the stall with his clothes on. He grabbed me in his arms and kissed me as I cried on his shoulder.

"What's wrong baby? What happened? Please talk to me. Please tell me what's going on. I need for YOU to tell me, Tisha." Jerrod said pleading with me to release that burden that was on my shoulders.

I looked up into his beautiful brown eyes as the water rained down on us and I felt complete. I felt like I could tell him anything and I didn't have to fear judgment. Before I knew it, I had spilled my guts as I cried and Jerrod held me tight. I told him about the beatings, and starvation, followed by the worst torture ever. I trembled in his arms as I described each sexual encounter with Jerome. When I began to describe what they did to me the night he found me, Jerrod sobbed and begged me to stop.

"Please baby, please. You don't have to say another word. I'm gonna kill them muthafuckas, Tisha. TISHHAAA, I'm so sorry baby. I couldn't protect you. Baby, I'm so sorry. I'ma make 'em pay, Tisha. I promise you, baby. I love you, Tisha." Jerrod said crying as snot, tears, and water streamed down his face.

I grabbed his face and kissed him deeply as I cried with him. After a few minutes, he whisked me up in his arms and carried me out of the shower. I grabbed a towel off the rack by the door and wiped away his and my tears before using it to cover myself. Jerrod carried me out of the bathroom and back to his room, laying me softly on the bed. After getting dressed, he and I sat in the bed and ate pizza while watching a movie, just enjoying each other's presence. We watched movie after movie wrapped in each other's arms until it was well after 10 p.m. I fell asleep on Jerrod's shoulder and woke up at about 2:30 a.m. to find him gone. I searched the house, but there was no sign of Jerrod so I sat on the couch in the living room and turned on the TV. After about ten minutes of infomercials, I fell and woke up to Jerrod bumping my leg. I opened my eyes and looked at him as he stood there frozen with blood splattered all over him and a terrified expression on his face like he had seen a ghost.

"Baby, what's wrong? What happened, Jerrod?" I asked him as a single tear fell from his eye as he huffed and puffed while biting his bottom lip.

"I took care of it, baby. I made sure he would never hurt you or anybody else again. I love you, Tisha." Jerrod said as my heart dropped into my feet.

I knew right then that Jerrod had killed Jerome and that things were about to change drastically. I held on to Jerrod and rubbed his head as he sobbed on my shoulder. There was my king, my knight in shining armor, hurting and needing a little help, and I was determined to be there for him. I told Jerrod how much I loved him and that we had to pull things together. I escorted him into his room to gather some clothes and money then told him to get the keys to Keith's car. I stood by the door and waited as Jerrod went into the room and argued with Keith to take the car. After a punch and two slams on the ground, Keith's selfish ass finally gave Jerrod the keys and we left, headed to a hotel.

"I'ma take you to the room first then I'll go back to the hood and get Terricka. We gone be straight as long as we're all together. I told you I got you and I won't let anything happen to you." Jerrod said as he drove down Thomas headed into downtown.

He got us a suite at the Marriot and then walked me up to the room before leaving to go get Terricka. I thought about Jerrod risking his freedom, life, and future for me as I sat in the huge King sized bed, staring at the TV. In no time Jerrod was back with Terricka and Buddy, food, weed, and alcohol, turning our hide out into party central. We all ate, smoked, laughed, and had fun until late in the night. I fell asleep in the king sized bed next to Jerrod happy and content, blocking out the darkness that loomed over us.

Chapter 10

For two weeks Jerrod, Terricka, Buddy, and I lived in our suite at the Marriott on the fourth floor, secluded from the rest of the world. The only time any of us left the room was to get food, weed, or buy new clothes. We were in our own little world, void of the pain and despair we had grown accustomed to.

On the first of March, Terricka and Buddy decided that it was time for them to hit the trap to get more money, leaving Jerrod and I in the room alone. We hadn't been alone since I first went home with him so I was very nervous of what would happen.

After all of the sexual violations I had experienced since my mother decided to be a madam, I still felt shy and uncertain when I thought about making love to Jerrod. I laid in the king sized bed, watching the Wendy Williams show as Jerrod locked the door behind Terricka and Buddy. When he came back over to the bed, he jumped on my back causing me to squeal as he tickled my sides.

"Say you love me and I'm the master." Jerrod said as he tickled me until I turned over on to my back.

I laughed and begged him to stop as he began a combination of tickles and kisses all over my face.

"I love you and you're the master." I said giggling as Jerrod laughed and fell on top of me.

Suddenly, our fit of giggles stopped as Jerrod's lips touched mine, igniting a fire and desire deep inside of me I didn't know existed. Jerrod and I kissed hard, fast, and passionately, running our fingers through each other's hair as we gazed at one another lovingly. I could feel his manhood growing between my legs and the thought of him inside of me both scared and excited me. I was afraid because every sexual experience I had up until that point was horrible. I was scared that I wouldn't know what to do with someone who was touching me because they loved me and not just to use me.

A million thoughts and worries ran through my head as I laid beneath the man of my dreams and he kissed me down my neck to my breasts. I jumped when Jerrod raised up the white wife beater I had on with nothing underneath and licked my nipple before blowing on it. The sensation of his cool, wet tongue on my sensitive breasts sent jolts all through my body and I felt my vagina get wet. I wanted to be with Jerrod despite my fears. I wanted to be with him forever and always have his love.

"Baby, I'll stop if you want me to. I'll do whatever you want, Tisha" Jerrod panted as I shook my head and told him not to stop.

With those words Jerrod slowly and gently pulled my top over my head and threw it on the floor before grabbing my 42DD breasts in his hands and kissing them both. He took my right breast into his mouth and sucked gently while grinding his hips, pressing his penis into my clitoris. I moaned and bit my bottom lip as pleasure and happiness overcame me and I reached up to pull Jerrod's shirt off. Within minutes, we had all of our clothes off and Jerrod was back between my legs kissing me deeply and looking into my eyes.

"I love you, Tisha, and I want to do this, and I don't have no rubbers. Are you sure you still want to do this? I know you clean and so am I, but do you want to take a chance with pregnancy? Me, I'd be happy to have you as my wife and the mother of my children. It's up to you though, baby." Jerrod said as he kissed my neck before looking into my eyes again.

I thought about everything he said and saw flashes of him and I happily married with three beautiful kids. I knew that if I was to have a baby with him it would be taken care of and loved by two great parents. I couldn't think of anyone in the world I would rather do something so serious as to have a baby with, other than Jerrod.

I looked into Jerrod's eyes as tears ran down my face and I kissed him deeply before grabbing his manhood in my hand and guiding it inside of me. Jerrod entered me gently and easily, slipping into my sea of wetness and just staying there. It was like his penis was made to fit my vagina because they fit perfectly together like pieces of a puzzle. Jerrod was so gentle and intense as he slowly dug deep inside of me with his 10 inch penis and his juicy, magical lips left love all over my face, neck, and breasts. His touch felt so good that I melted in his embrace. We thrust our bodies together in rhythm as I cried tears of joy and Jerrod kissed them off of my face as they fell. We made love for hours as Jerrod made me see ecstasy over and over again. When the waves of euphoria that had us on cloud nine subsided, Jerrod and I laid there in each other's arms, spent and filled with nothing but love.

For the two and a half weeks following that day, Jerrod and I were wrapped up in a web of love. We were like bees to honey, you couldn't find Jerrod unless I was right there with him. I experienced nothing but happiness until I began to feel sick every morning. Even when feeling nauseas and having back pains, Jerrod was still able to brighten my day and keep me happy. Happiness was all I knew until one day everything fell apart.

It was March 18th, exactly one month before Terricka's 18th birthday, when my world got flipped upside down once again. We were still living out of the room and Terricka, and I had went downtown to shop before coming back to the hotel and finding our room still dirty. After going to speak with housekeeping and having a small dispute, Terricka and I stepped outside to smoke while they cleaned the room. When we got back in the room, everything appeared to be normal as the housekeepers apologized before leaving and we inspected the room. Everything looked great so we sat down to smoke a blunt and chill before the boys got back.

As soon as I lit the blunt, there was a knock at the door and the hair on the back of my neck stood up. It was like I knew something was about to happen. I knew that if we opened that door there would be no turning back. I put out the blunt and grabbed the weed to go flush it as someone yelled housekeeping on the other side of the door. I shook my head telling Terricka not to answer the door on my way to the bathroom, but she brushed me off. I was flushing the last little bit of weed down the toilet when I heard the door fly open and someone yelled, "MPD!" as Terricka yelled and cursed. I came out of the bathroom with my hands on my head and got down on my knees and interlocked my ankles. I knew the routine as the police grabbed me and handcuffed me as they informed my sister and me that we had warrants.

The ride to Juvenile Court was quiet as the females cop tried to make small talk with us, but we ignored her ass. We didn't want to hear shit she had to say. After getting processed into the system, I asked for my one phone call and called Mrs. Cunningham for help. I told her everything as I sobbed into the phone and begged her to get the charges dropped because we were defending ourselves. She agreed to help and to use the influence her husband, the DA, had to get us off and into the same foster home as our brother. Within four days, Mrs. Cunningham and her husband were at juvenile picking us up and taking us to this big blue house out in the heart of Bartlett. It was in the middle of nowhere with nothing but fields and flowers everywhere. It was the field in my dreams, the place I imagined when I wanted to escape reality.

When Terricka and I got out of the car, we were greeted by a healthy, happy Sha who jumped into our arms and let us plant kisses all over his face. We were happier than we had ever been as we loved on our brother and then met the rest of our temporary family. Their names were the Robinson's and the heads of the family were the mom and dad, Tania and Michael. They had three children; a daughter named, Krista, who was nineteen years old; a daughter named, Jewel, who was fifteen years old; and a son named, Ryan, who was seven years old. The Robinson's were the happiest, perkiest, up-beat black people we had ever seen. I instantly feel in love with them and adapted to their home very quickly. Everything was like paradise once again. Until one day, I woke up to the worst stomach pains ever. I went into the bathroom and tried to use it but nothing came out no matter how much I pushed.

I moaned in pain and rocked on the toilet hoping the pain would soon end. Suddenly, the door flew open and Krista crept in with something behind her back as she offered her help.

"I know what you're going through right now so you don't even have to say nothing. I been right there in the same position I can tell you right now that you're pregnant because I can see it in your face, nose, and titties. However, if you don't believe me, all you have to do is pee on this stick." Krista said putting the pregnancy test she had behind her back into my hand.

I did what Krista said as tears streamed down my cheeks and then sat and talked to her about Jerrod as we waited on the results. I told her how I hadn't talked to him since everything happened and that I wished I could find him, but I didn't have the number anymore. Krista consoled me as I cried about the love I couldn't find when suddenly the timer we set went off. I got up on shaky legs and looked at the test to see two blue lines. It was just like Krista said, I was pregnant. I cried and asked Krista to help me find him as she helped me out of the bathroom.

"I got you now. Go back to bed and get some rest." Krista said as I hugged her before going to my room.

The next day Krista fulfilled her promise and found the new number and address on Keith via Facebook. After taking me to Birth Right and finding out I was six weeks pregnant, Krista took me back home so I could begin my search for the father of my unborn child. I couldn't help but to think something was wrong with Jerrod for not trying to contact me because I knew he loved me too much to just let me go. I cried as I thought about the time we spent together looking at the number and address in my hand.

I called the number a dozen times as I dressed and prepared to go back to the hood to find Jerrod. I let the phone ring twenty times each time I called, but there still was no answer.

I left my foster home walking that day, April 1st at about 2:45 in the afternoon. By 4:30 I was getting off the bus in Hickory Hill headed to Keith's new apartment in 6111 Crossing, a new apartment complex.

I knocked on the door and waited, rubbing my stomach as I heard someone scurry to the door. When Keith opened the door, I felt relief knowing that I had at least found Jerrod's house and I was one step closer to being back with him. I asked Keith where Jerrod was with a big smile on my face, expecting a happy answer. Instead Keith looked as if his life had ended as he told me he didn't know.

"I don't know where he is. We haven't seen him in a month. His homies said he went missing the same night you and your sister got locked up.

We been searching everywhere and we can't find him, Tisha. We don't know if he dead or what." Keith said as a tear streamed down his face. I felt as if all of the life had been sucked out of my body as I held my stomach and my legs gave out.

Keith was right there to catch me as I cried and told him I was pregnant with Jerrod's baby. Keith helped me into the house and cried on my shoulder as he told me it would be okay. I sat there for a while wondering where my love could be before Keith told me I didn't look so good and asked if he could take me to a hospital or home. I agreed to go home because I knew that I needed to rest and not cause any more stress to my growing baby. The entire ride back to Bartlett I cried as Keith promised he would find his brother and help me in any way that I needed it.

By the time I made it home, I was all cried out and emotionally drained as Keith helped me on the porch before kissing my cheek, and going back to his car.

"I promise we'll find him, Tisha, and we will help with the baby." Keith said to me before pulling off.

I watched him disappear down the driveway before taking a deep breath and entering the house. When I stepped inside, I instantly knew something was wrong because the aura felt different, there was some evil nearby and I could feel it. When I walked into the kitchen and saw my mother sitting at the island with my foster mother all dressed up for one of her stellar performances, sipping tea like high society, I knew my fairy tale was over. There was Denise, the enforcer of pain, the dark cloud that pummeled me with storms all of my life. It was then that I knew my fight had just begun.

THE END

If you're interested in becoming an author for True Glory Publications, please send three completed chapters for your manuscript to Truegloypublications@gmail.com

Thanks for your interest!

Here are more True Glory Publications release links available on Amazon.

Tiffany Stephens
Expect the Unexpected Part 1
http://www.amazon.com/Expect-Unexpected-Tiffany-Stephens-ebook/dp/B00J84URUM/ref=sr_1_1?ie=UTF8&qid=14135 70346&sr=8-1&keywords=TIFFANY+STEPHENS
Expect the Unexpected Part 2
http://www.amazon.com/Expect-Unexpected-2-Tiffany-Stephens-ebook/dp/B00LHCCYG8/ref=sr_1_2?ie=UTF8&qid=1413 570346&sr=8-2&keywords=TIFFANY+STEPHENS

Kim Morris: Tears I Shed Part 1 & 2
http://www.amazon.com/Tears-I-Shed-Kim-Morris/dp/1499319800

http://www.amazon.com/Tears-I-Shed-2-ebook/dp/B00N4FD03C

Sha Cole
Her Mother's Love Part 1

http://www.amazon.com/Her-Mothers-love-Sha-Cole-ebook/dp/B00H93Z03I/ref=sr_1_1?s=digital-text&ie=UTF8&qid=1405463882&sr=1-1&keywords=her+mothers+love

Her Mother's Love Part 2

http://www.amazon.com/HER-MOTHERS-LOVE-Sha-Cole-ebook/dp/B00IKBGWW6/ref=pd_sim_kstore_1?ie=UTF8&refRID=1EFA9EPXRPBSQPZVWHM0

Her Mother's Love Part 3

http://www.amazon.com/Her-Mothers-Love-Sha-Cole-ebook/dp/B00L2SHLNI/ref=pd_sim_kstore_1?ie=UTF8&refRID=1AW831PBNBGAPPP9G8A9

Guessing Game

http://www.amazon.com/Guessing-Game-Sha-Cole-ebook/dp/B00ODST1AA/ref=sr_1_8?ie=UTF8&qid=1413041318&sr=8-8&keywords=Sha+Cole

Niki Jilvontae
A Broken Girl's Journey
http://www.amazon.com/BROKEN-GIRLS-JOURNEY-Niki-Jilvontae-ebook/dp/B00IICJRQK/ref=sr_1_5?ie=UTF8&qid=1413419382&sr=8-5&keywords=niki+jilvontae

A Broken Girl's Journey 2
http://www.amazon.com/BROKEN-GIRLS-JOURNEY-ebook/dp/B00J9ZM9YW/ref=sr_1_4?ie=UTF8&qid=1413419382&sr=8-4&keywords=niki+jilvontae

A Broken Girl's Journey 3

http://www.amazon.com/BROKEN-GIRLS-JOURNEY-ebook/dp/B00JVDFTBM/ref=sr_1_1?ie=UTF8&qid=1413419382&sr=8-1&keywords=niki+jilvontae

A Broken Girl's Journey 4: Kylie's Song
http://www.amazon.com/Broken-Girls-Journey-Kylies-Song-ebook/dp/B00NK89604/ref=sr_1_6?ie=UTF8&qid=1413419382&sr=8-6&keywords=niki+jilvontae

A Long Way from Home
http://www.amazon.com/Long-Way-Home-Niki-Jilvontae-ebook/dp/B00LCN252U/ref=sr_1_3?ie=UTF8&qid=1413419382&sr=8-3&keywords=niki+jilvontae

Your Husband, My Man Part 2 KC Blaze

http://www.amazon.com/Your-Husband-Man-YOUR-HUSBAND-ebook/dp/B00MUAKRPQ/ref=sr_1_1?ie=UTF8&qid=1413593158&sr=8-1&keywords=your+husband+my+man+2

Your Husband, My Man Part 3 KC Blaze

http://www.amazon.com/Your-Husband-My-Man-3-ebook/dp/B00OJODI8Y/ref=sr_1_1?ie=UTF8&qid=14135

93252&sr=8-

1&keywords=your+husband+my+man+3+kc+blaze

Child of a Crackhead I Shameek Speight

http://www.amazon.com/CHILD-CRACKHEAD-Part-1-

ebook/dp/B0049U4W56/ref=sr_1_1?s=digital-

text&ie=UTF8&qid=1413594876&sr=1-

1&keywords=child+of+a+crackhead

Child of a Crackhead II Shameek Speight

http://www.amazon.com/CHILD-CRACKHEAD-II-

Shameek-Speight-

ebook/dp/B004MME12K/ref=sr_1_2?ie=UTF8&qid=1413

593375&sr=8-2&keywords=child+of+a+crackhead+series

Pleasure of Pain Part 1 Shameek Speight

http://www.amazon.com/Pleasure-pain-Shameek-Speight-ebook/dp/B005C68BE4/ref=sr_1_1?s=digital-text&ie=UTF8&qid=1413593888&sr=1-1&keywords=pleasure+of+pain

Infidelity at its Finest Part 1 Kylar Bradshaw

http://www.amazon.com/INFIDELITY-AT-ITS-FINEST-Book-ebook/dp/B00HV539A0/ref=sr_1_sc_1?s=digital-text&ie=UTF8&qid=1413595045&sr=1-1-spell&keywords=Infideltiy+at+its+finest

Infidelity at its Finest Part 2 Kylar Bradshaw

http://www.amazon.com/Infidelity-Finest-Part-Kylar-Bradshaw-ebook/dp/B00IORHGNA/ref=sr_1_2?s=digital-text&ie=UTF8&qid=1413593700&sr=1-2&keywords=infidelity+at+its+finest

Marques Lewis
It's Love For Her part 1 http://www.amazon.com/Its-Love-Her-Marques-Lewis-

ebook/dp/B00KAQAI1A/ref=la_B00B0GACDI_1_3?s=bo
oks&ie=UTF8&qid=1413647892&sr=1-3

It's Love For Her 2   http://www.amazon.com/Its-Love-For-
Her-
ebook/dp/B00KXLGG5O/ref=pd_sim_b_1?ie=UTF8&refR
ID=1ABE9DSRTHFFH13WGH6E

It's Love For Her 3 http://www.amazon.com/Its-Love-For-
Her-
ebook/dp/B00NUOIP0A/ref=pd_sim_kstore_1?ie=UTF8&
refRID=1PYKVRTJJJMYCHE0P5RQ

Words of Wetness   http://www.amazon.com/Words-
Wetness-Marques-Lewis-
ebook/dp/B00MMQT2OU/ref=pd_sim_kstore_2?ie=UTF8
&refRID=1FJFWTZSN2DBCV6PX3MG

He Loves Me to Death Sonovia Alexander
http://www.amazon.com/HE-LOVES-DEATH-LOVE-
Book-
ebook/dp/B00I2E1ARI/ref=sr_1_1?s=books&ie=UTF8&qi
d=1416789703&sr=1-1&keywords=sonovia+alexander

Silent Cries Sonovia Alexander
http://www.amazon.com/Silent-Cries-Sonovia-Alexander-
ebook/dp/B00FANSOEQ/ref=sr_1_6?s=books&ie=UTF8&
qid=1416789941&sr=1-
6&keywords=sonovia+alexander+silent+cries

Ghetto Love Sonovia Alexander
http://www.amazon.com/GHETTO-LOVE-Sonovia-
Alexander-
ebook/dp/B00GK5AP5O/ref=sr_1_5?s=books&ie=UTF8&
qid=1416790164&sr=1-
5&keywords=sonovia+alexander+ghetto+love

Robert Cost
Every Bullet Gotta Name Part 1
http://www.amazon.com/dp/B00SU7KJ7O
Every Bullet Gotta Name Part 2
http://www.amazon.com/dp/B00TE7PSGG

CPSIA information can be obtained
at www.ICGtesting.com
Printed in the USA
LVHW012322250720
661537LV00021B/2345